Dedicated to Jill Wendy Wood

And to my daughter, Evie Harper Wood.

By C.S.WOOD

SABRE

Part I

The Shattered Oath

Part II

The Rise of the Night Devil

Part III

The Mark of the Veleth

C.S.WOOD

SABRE ©

PART I

THE SHATTERED OATH

C.S.WOOD

First published 2023 by Compass-Publishing UK

ISBN 978-1-915962-25-6
Copyright © C.S.Wood, 2023

Edited and typeset by C.S.Wood

Cover design by C.S.Wood

A CIP catalogue record for this book is available from the British Library.

Printed and bound by Maxim UK Ltd

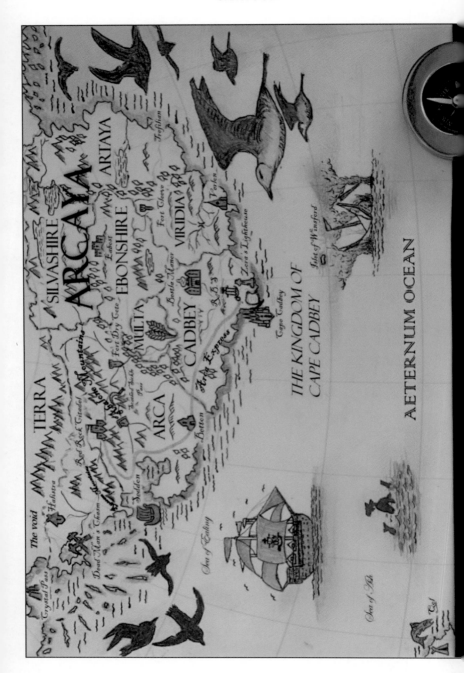

A map showing the Kingdoms of Cape Cadbey and Merithia, and the eastern shores of Sundrithia. The desert expanses of Sundrith and the eastern reaches of Scavana are not shown. Certified 1803 by the R.B.S cartographer, Wilbert O'Hara.

C.S.WOOD

Chapter 1
The Night Devil

Sweat slithered down the captain's nose and a heavy heart raged against his chest. A vault door stood before him and two royal marines. Its iron components looked impenetrable, but in thirty seconds time these locks would no longer exist. Their eyes remained fixed on a pocket watch. A successful raid would bring valour and honour, for this was a Skua raid led by its most lethal detachment, Sabre Squadron.

The Royal Skuas were an elite naval force, designed to intercept and eliminate enemy ships. They were guardians loyal to the Kingdom of Cape Cadbey; invasion fleet interceptors; Royal Boat Service marines; night devils. Devils go by many names…

"Ten seconds," the captain grunted to his two companions. Their black trench coats and ponchos had merged with the darkness. Bicorn hats extended before them like harrowing beaks; their frayed edges resembled wings. Bandannas masked their scowling faces; only their piercing eyes glinted in the gloom. "Stand by!" he said. Gloved hands clutched their revolvers.

"Five, F-" An almighty explosion spewed metal down the corridor! A billow of smoke consumed them.

"Premature as usual, Jared!" Robert coughed, whilst brushing debris from his poncho. He was the largest of the three marines and took most of the blast. Within seconds, alarm bells began ringing. The Skuas dashed inside the vault and began loading their sacks with gold.

"Two minutes and then we move on the dot," the captain ordered, for a regiment of guards would be on their way.

"Jared, you wanted a gift for Ness. See if she likes this," said Robert, before tossing him a broken hand mirror. Jared stated it had been damaged in the blast. Robert laughed and shouted, "Her face would've cracked it anyway!"

"I'll tell her you said that."

"Hurry, hurry now," their captain stressed.

"You're surrounded. Come out with your hands in the air!" came a stern voice from outside the vault.

The Skua captain remained calm, checked his watch, and said, "Absurd, two minutes hasn't passed yet. Jared, stick your 'ead around that door and tell 'em ta wait!" The captain threw Jared his pistol, which he clasped from the air. "Rob, keep filling those bags!" Jared took position beside the smouldering entry.

"We know who you are, vile night devils," the voice continued. "That gold belongs to the unified peoples of Sundrithia[1]. Lay down your weapons..." As commanded, Jared opened fire. Bullet casings leapt across the floor as brick work exploded into dust. Shots ricocheted off the iron door, whilst their captain examined the vault's furthest wall. Another minute passed.

"Captain!?" Robert bellowed, as he continued sacking gold. Gunfire resonated around them.

Then, when hope was fading, their captain shouted, "Seal those bags. Jared, say your goodbyes and close that door. Time to leave." Fretting, Jared abandoned his position and pushed the contraption shut. They were sealed in a tomb of riches, until their captain stepped back to reveal another bomb. The blast singed their coats.

"A warning would have been nice, captain," Robert spluttered through his sleeve. The three crusaders clambered into a crumbling sewer and sprinted through its stench, their

---

[1] Lands claimed by High Sheik Kabil on the eastern shores of Sundrith.

coats flailing behind them. Eventually, they reached an opening where the tunnel began to narrow. Cannons bellowed in the distance, as if the sea were a demon. The coast was being shelled.

"Flare!" Jared quickly fired a signal out the opening. The red light fizzed and twirled above a meringue of ocean. Then, a skimmer boat labelled HMS Sabre appeared in the open. The captain ordered everyone to jump aboard the revolutionary attack vessel, which was powered by steam and the wonders of hycinthium-lapis[2]. Rob, being the largest of the three, was the only sailor to hesitate. He eventually followed with a thud that rocked the vehicle.

"Nice of you to join us," the skipper hailed, as waves lapped the side of her ship. The Skuas recognised her as Spike. Night had consumed the confines of her cabin and cockpit.

"Captain, I should have known you'd have an ace up your sleeve," Jared huffed in relief, as he threw himself into a seat at the stern, beside a large gun emplacement. Their skimmer took off under the cover of nightfall, leaving the vaults of Fort Thindraka[3] behind it. The sailors began celebrating. Any feelings of anxiety had been eradicated by the gold that fell between their fingers. The smell of coin was intoxicating.

"Another successful raid, captain," said Rob. "Wait until the mothership hears about this! Did you know that sewer was there?" But then, in the distance, several gunshots echoed. Their captain dropped to his knees. All laughter ceased, as Robert broke his fall. Then, three cannons howled from the shoreline.

"INCOMING!" Jared screamed, as their ship banked to the left and then to the right! Cannon balls screeched from the sky, forcing the ocean to erupt around them. More shots fell in the distance, until they were clear of danger. Jared pleaded for

---

[2] A charged stone found amongst the treacherous chasms and infamous mines of Terra province.

[3] A citadel on the eastern shores of Sundrith.

their captain to 'say something', as Rob lay him down beside blood splattered sacks of gold.

"How the hell did they hit us?" Spike yelled from her cabin. Scarlet hands squirmed to stop the bleeding, but it was already too late.

"He's dead, Jared. Jared, he's dead. There's nothing we can do," said Rob in despair. Their captain had been shot through the chest. Pieces of his heart had plastered Jared's trench coat. All the gold in the world was not worth their loss.

"This does not happen... This is *not allowed* to happen!" Jared scrunched his bicorn hat and threw it at the floor. Their boat cut through the swell towards the silhouette of a galleon. Starlight, endangered by mist, revealed an array of daunting sails. Sabre Squadron feared what awaited them, now their captain was dead. Eventually, they were side by side with the mothership. Two large chains were lowered, which Jared hooked into place at the ends of their vessel, so it could be winched from the waves. Their ascent felt like an eternity.

"How many bags?" a loud, gruff voice asked, as their boat reached the top. They found themselves upon a crowded deck, surrounded by hissing crimson lamps. Impenetrable clouds prevented the moon from glistening.

"Commander Grenyard," said Jared. He disembarked and saluted. "We lost our captain-"

"I might be blind in one eye," Grenyard replied. "But I see all. How many bags of gold did Fort Thindraka produce?"

Grenyard resembled death. His deep scars harboured the darkness. The splinters in his bones made him a part of the ship. An eye patch hid further horrors, and night spared them the worst of his appearance. Grenyard was feared for his cruelty. He had been a fearless captain, and a ruthless commander, but in recent months his actions had become savage.

"Four bags... and five pouches, sir," said Robert who was heartbroken. A silent jury surrounded them. Despite their captain's death, this was not a usual gathering. Every Skua seemed unified in dread. Another tragedy must have stricken the ship during the raid.

"I would have expected more, to account for the captain's failure," said Grenyard, causing Rob to gulp behind his bandanna. "Take his body down below. We sail north under my command!" Some cheered at the prospect of returning home. Many remained silent in remorse and disbelief. Questions had been raised regarding the legality and sanity of a raid on Fort Thindraka. It was as if Grenyard had intended for casualties to occur. Ness appeared from a dispersing crowd.

"Tell me it's not true," she whimpered.

She was wrapped in a trench coat and fighting a chill. A vile breeze fondled her long, blood-red hair, which caressed her bandanna. Her emerald eyes reflected a handheld lantern. Shaken, Jared nodded, before slowly embracing her. Then, he questioned why the crew were so agitated.

"You've not heard?" said Ness. "Vice admiral Leonard has vanished during the raid, or worse." The wind caused the sails to whisper, as Jared's stomach turned.

"Did he board one of the skimmers?" Rob asked. Several boats had attacked Fort Thindraka. Theirs had been the last to return following a successful breach. Ness shook her head. Confusion had plagued the ship. Worse yet, Commander Grenyard was now in charge.

The ship's surgeon approached them, as their captain's corpse was hoisted aboard. Spike barged past in anger and disappeared down deck. The others knew there was nothing they could say to calm her fury.

"Is that who I think it is?" the surgeon asked.

"Yes," Robert answered. "It's the body of Captain Thomas Witherow."

***

A boy jabbed his finger in the air and answered, "The year 1603!"

"Well done, Todd," said Mr Sweeney in delight. His enthusiastic voice echoed off the walls of a cavernous classroom. Todd could spend hours engrossed in history. Stories painted heroic images of how the Royal Skuas had saved kings and queens from assassination. Brave men and women had sacrificed everything to protect the Kingdom of Cape Cadbey. Yet, most people were captivated by the art of invention; a trend fuelled by a revolution of machines. But Todd was not destined to be an inventor. Machines terrified him, their fumes upset him, and maths caused his mind to wander. He had tried dismembering contraptions with his father, but he could never put them back together again.

Mr Sweeney continued, "Exactly two hundred years ago, in 1603, on this very day, a Merithian invasion fleet set sale for Cape Cadbey." Todd loved a good story about Merithia[4]: Cadbey's historical nemesis. But he flinched when a paper ball struck the back of his head. He turned in his seat to see Walter Spindler smirking. The boy was a pig and a bigot in the making. Walter bullied Todd for many reasons: his shortness, freckles, and enthusiasm; for starters. Walter even disliked him for having fair, shoulder length hair. Unfortunately, Todd looked young for his age. His dad would say, 'You're yet ta sprout, lad,' but Todd struggled to believe him. His hazel eyes beamed with innocence, and girls paid him no attention. Sweeney's chalk-stick tap-danced across the black board.

"Major Winsford sailed out to sea alone and pitched camp on, what is now known as, the Islet of Winsford. There, he spotted the enemy armada, and took note of their formation." Another projectile hit Todd, who jolted in frustration. This

---

[4] Merithia is a kingdom in the southern hemisphere spanning the continent of Scavana. It is ruled by Tsar Alva Olander of Artrik.

alerted the other children, who had been drugged with boredom.

"Is everything alright, Mr Witherow?" Sweeney asked. Todd gave a reluctant nod, as the other children sniggered.

"Very good," Sweeney concluded. The teacher was animated for his age. His hands conducted lessons like a symphony. Hyperactivity had kept him tall and thin. A prickly moustache matched his grey hair, and his tweed suit was always padded in chalk.

Sweeney continued, "Major Winsford was able to alert Cadbey by carrier pigeon. If the history books are to be believed, Winsford called for the deployment of his majesty's Royal Boat Service or R.B.S for short. However, scribbled at the bottom of his letter were the words: '*The Royal Skuas*'. Legend has it that Winsford, through his telescope, observed an enemy captain out on the ship's deck. He was preparing his breakfast, a boiled egg to be precise. Just as he was about to tuck in, a seabird swooped down and stole the egg!" Some children laughed. Others showed a lack of appreciation. "The seabird was a skua. So, if legend *is* to be believed, that is where the noble Skuas gained their nickname."

Major Winsford had realised the dire need for a quick response unit. Twice, Merithia had blockaded Cadbey, threatening its existence, but Queen Isabella's forces had prevailed throughout the 16th century. Nevertheless, the kingdom would not withstand a third siege. So, in the late 1500s, Winsford devised a crew. These brave men and women would sail agile ships capable of intercepting the enemy. His elite unit were trained to be fearless, unhesitant, and unwavering. One marine could take on a hundred enemy sailors. However, Winsford lacked a symbol for his daring cutthroats. Skuas swarmed Cadbey's coastline. These predatory seabirds could be seen pursuing other gulls, to make them disgorge any fish they had captured. The R.B.S had adopted similar tactics once its ships had finally dominated the Aeternum Ocean. Resolute, its sailors would raid enemy installations or ships for the greater good of the kingdom. The skua became their banner, but the unit had gained more sinister names.

"Sweeney!" A stern man had appeared in the doorway. It was headmaster, Johnathan Ackerley. His appearance was pristine in comparison to Sweeney's. A fine, oxblood vest jacket and tailcoat suited his authority. A white cravat portrayed his wealth. Lustrous black hair spiralled past his frown. Many thought Ackerley was too young for his profession, but he was well educated, confident and tenacious.

Professor Langley Stewart lingered behind him. He was not a teacher but a famous scientist, who had lifted Cadbey from the dark ages. His mind was responsible for every innovation powered by the wonders of hycinthium-lapis. A white periwig set him apart. Finned eyebrows arched towards his slender nose, which overhung his pursed lips and dimpled chin. His youthful face was cleanshaven and powdered.

"I thought we had discussed your drearings about fables and seabirds," Ackerley shouted. Tasselled boots carried him inside the classroom.

Sweeney clapped his hands and said, "Mr Ackerley, how nice of you to join us. I was making sure I had their full attention by adding a little humour to the equation."

"Humour, eh?" Ackerley examined the black board. "Tell me… will humour build the next engine… or aid us in the invention of the flying machine?"

"Not unless it's powered on laughs, sir," Mr Sweeney joked.

"Will it rid our streets of disease and poverty?" He made his way over to Todd, who looked worried. Their eyes met. Mr Ackerley recognised Todd as being the son of ex-vice admiral and knight of the realm, Sir Alan Witherow.

"No, sir," said Sweeney.

"And will humour, legends, myths or Skuas for that matter, see the kingdom through the interregnum ahead?" Ackerley was referring to his dream of a revolution; a movement that would end the monarchy. Langley scoffed in amusement, as Ackerley awaited a response.

Sweeney paused and bit his lip before answering, "Well, they saw us through the last one." Ackerley shouted Sweeney's name in disapproval, which caused the children to jump. Todd gulped, as the headmaster discovered a paper ball at his feet. He unravelled it to reveal a picture of Todd being messed on by seabirds.

"Sweeney, you have one week to submit a new ninety-day lesson plan focused on inventions through time. I don't want to hear another word about the bloody Skuas. Do I make myself clear?" Ackerley checked his pocket watch and left the room, as if he and Langley were late for an appointment. Mr Sweeney gave Todd a sombre look and apologised.

Seabirds screeched high above a bustling playground, where concrete mirrored a dismal sky. Autumn had bled into winter. Tumbling ashen clouds would disperse, but not until the children had been summoned back inside. Todd had found refuge in a history book beside the perimeter wall. A sea breeze fed his lungs and lifted his fringe.

"Look, it's bird crap boy!" Walter shouted, before slapping the book from Todd's hands. Walter had invited his henchman, Hugh, who was another cumbersome toad.

"You're an idiot, Spindler. What does that even mean?" Todd shouted. His courage exceeded his stature.

"It means you love birds so much; you live in their mess!" Walter spat, which made his cheeks wobble, and his beady eyes squint.

His belly strained the buttons of his patched vest jacket. Walter's suffering mother could not afford to properly dress her expanding son. Scarfs warmed their necks, and scuffed shoes and ripped shorts covered their lower halves.

"I respect the Skuas and so should you!" Todd pointed at a shield emblem above the school's entrance. It depicted the silhouette of a Skua: a large seabird swooping in for the steal. Three jagged waves formed its base, and three vertical pikes formed its backdrop, which glinted in the autumn sun. The words 'Royal Boat Service' were in a banner below the logo. Top centre was a royal crown, which featured another banner stating intercipere, propulso, prōvidēre or intercept, eliminate, provide. Its features were proud and robust.

"My dad said the Skuas are a bunch of pirates and rapist thieves," Walter argued.

"Your brother included," said Hugh in a sly manner. Todd missed his brother dearly, despite envying his role as a Skua captain. The duo had crossed the line.

"Leave my family out of this!" Todd screamed, before booting Hugh in the crotch. The bully staggered to the floor in excruciating pain. Walter attempted his signature move, a bear hug, but his target was too fast. Todd ducked out of reach, reclaimed his book, and sprinted through the crowd.

Hugh and Walter would report him. Helpless, Todd had no choice but to run. He rushed down a back alley, past a group of smokers and through a gap in the fence. Then, he dashed downhill leaving the school behind him.

The Kingdom of Cape Cadbey lay before him. A colossal cape extended south into a glistening ocean. Many had likened it to the shape of a dagger. At its tip stood a beautiful cathedral bathed in a thin mist. Four towers, boasting spires as white as marble, pierced the heavens. They formed the corners of a rooftop courtyard, outlined with steeples. An apex roof, a grand rose window, and gigantic arched doors formed its front. High walls and four turrets shielded its magnificence. Cannons peered from their nests, as seabirds powered a looming vortex of cloud. In the comfort of its shadow lay the market district. This vibrant hub sold produce from all over Cadbey's eight provinces, which spanned the continent of Arcaya[5]. Many lopsided houses had been crammed into this busy area, where merchants filled the streets. Cadbey's

---

[5]An arched shaped continent covering the northern hemisphere. Arcaya means arch of the world.

residents enjoyed being close to God, trade, honest work, and they no longer feared the prospect of a seaborne invasion. Slate roofs reflected a timid sun. Chimneys puffed smoke into a veil of smog, whilst gothic architecture and sculptures sustained the citadel's beauty. Pulsing paths connected the cathedral to the palace - the heart of Cadbey - where King Oborus III resided. The palace overlooked Isabella's Square and a less chaotic business district, in the centre of the cape. Here, lords, entrepreneurs and inventors were investing their fortunes. Buildings in this sector were orderly, better spaced, and similar in design. Few could afford to live in the business district, but grand, town houses awaited those who could. Todd continued his rapid descent through piles of leaves. He would have to breach the citadel's walls if he were to reach his home in the market district. Towering stone faces and turrets, perpetual in their duty, observed the bay and the Aeternum Ocean.

A little further inland was the churn of the industrial sector, which had spread beyond the walls. Hexagonal chimneys and mills, built from red brick, exhaled smoke. A network of brass pipes and valves sweated. Todd's school was on the outskirts of this zone. It had been built on a hill to the east, to avoid being suffocated by pollution. Terraced houses stood on the same mound, where rows of washing had been hung out to dry, as checkpoints for Todd's excursion.

Waves twinkled in a large harbour, which dominated the bay. Strangely, a large galleon was approaching, but Todd could not stop to study its origin. 'Could it be a Skua warship?' he thought. Fishing boats were forced to avoid the ship's presence, where factories and jagged warehouses formed busy shipyards. They were home to a battalion of seabirds, who sought the stench of trawl. The bay was protected by a large concrete wall. This stone arm cut through the sea as if it had always been there. It was a defensive masterpiece that connected the cape to the east of the cove. A large gate, known as the King's Mouth, kept invaders out.

Slumbering cannons and guards had been angled towards the equator. Treacherous peaks protected the eastern bay, where Zora's[6] lighthouse loomed over the harbour, like a temple of fire. Her flame beacons roared, so sailors could find their way home. Further guns lined its verdant edges; a reminder that visitors were not welcome.

Little legs carried Todd home, whilst his stomach boiled a broth of exhilaration and regret. Eventually, he had no choice but to stop for breath.

"Calm down boy, you'll give yourself a heart attack!" a beggar joked from beside a fountain.

The old man resembled a piece of coral cast from the waves. His frayed beard had fused with a sheepskin blanket. A woollen tea-cosy warmed his head, but his crooked nose beat sore with cold. Warts had formed on his leathery skin beside sunspots, deep creases, and further blemishes earnt at sea. The beggar was known to Todd. He had often seen him drift past his window, as if the wanderer was drawn to his abode. The vagrant saw all and knew all. Todd kindly presented the beggar with his dinner money, but the man wagged his finger.

"I won't be needing it," Todd panted. The old man thought for a second, before gesturing the boy closer. Then, he thrust his blanket aside, to reveal a row of medals. "You were a Skua!?" Todd exclaimed. The old man shushed him quiet.

"Aye but keep it to yourself, lad. Should the Merithians come for me in me sleep!" An amusing wink was rejected by confusion. Todd did not understand. These medals were meant to be worn with pride, yet the Royal Skua was destitute and hiding in his own kingdom.

"They don't look after us the way they used to… That and these 'ere medals are all I have. Wouldn't want anyone nicking 'em now would I. Now, run along fella!" said the man.

---

[6] Zora is the brightest star in the northern hemisphere, named after the prophet Allód's mother.

Todd paused in thought. "That's an order, lad!" Todd nodded and took off into the distance.

He cut down an alleyway, plastered in circus and theatre posters, where he hurdled several connecting pipes. Then, the boy came to an abrupt stop, as a carrier drone scuttled across his path.

The arachnid machine was powered by the wonders of hycinthium-lapis; a charged stone recently discovered in the chasms of Terra[7] province. Carrier drones were restricted to the industrial sector, so Todd was surprised to see the metallic entity in his district. Four pointed feet clinked along the cobbles. Its pyramid head featured a human face on each side, meant to make drones more acceptable, yet their ghastly expressions haunted Todd's dreams. Each drone had been finetuned to navigate Cadbey's streets; but they were insentient, meaning they would often collide with houses, horses, and pedestrians. The world was not ready for many of Langley's inventions, nor was it ready for the power of Hycinthium-lapis. The drone scurried away, so Todd continued his journey.

Finally, he was home: a terraced house, along the centre of a narrow street, in the shadow of Hadley's Turret. He could see a soaring fortress wall and the turret his street was named after. On a clear day, Todd would climb the tower, so he could see his house from up high, and look out across the sea. A shiny black door, numbered twenty-two, invited him inside. Todd had not decided what he would tell his father if he was home. So, his stomach somersaulted when he realised his father was present. Stern voices rebounded down the narrow hallway. A grandfather clock chimed opposite the stairs, beside the kitchen door, allowing Todd to enter without being detected. A large painting, of a galleon at sea, covered the wall opposite the banister.

---

[7] An arctic province located in Arcaya.

"They have no business in the Sundrith[8] archipelagos. Those lands have never, ever, posed a threat to Cadbey. Skirmishes undertaken there should be illegal," said Todd's father, Alan Witherow. He was a well-respected veteran who had kept himself affiliated with the king's council.

"Why do you so ardently fight a band you served? They are your family. Your eldest son is out there right now flying the banner! Such words do not favour a man when they're aimed at his own kin," Arthur Shilling argued. "You should leave the nitty gritty to me."

Arthur was a powerful family friend, who held the position of minister for economics. He was also Todd's godfather. The boy cowered when he realised his kitchen had become an arena for politics. Shadows danced across the plaster as he listened in, without making the floorboards creek.

Alan said, "You have a brother. If your brother had been an accessory ta robbery n' murder, would ya not have him put before a judge for his crimes?"

Arthur sighed and replied, "The Skuas still act to serve the best interests of the kingdom. It will take more than accusations to drive reform."

"Nonsense...There's no smoke without fire," said Alan. "The Skuas are only acting to serve themselves. In the days of old we were driven by respect and valour. Now we have the seas, they're only driven by greed." Suddenly, their living room radiator began to kick. The crude contraption would often faulter, causing Alan to beat it. Todd hurried into the room, skidded onto his knees, and pulled its lever, before his father could react. A snaking element glowed, just beyond its cage. Todd sighed in relief. He preferred their fireplace, which stood opposite a bay window. Decorative carvings, and tiles showing painted goddesses, lined its sides. Nowadays, only webs floated above its forgotten ashes. Todd flinched, as a

---

[8] A continent of arid deserts. The Sundrith archipelagos and its jungles are located to the south.

drinking globe, Alan's oxblood armchair, and several bookshelves flickered from view. A hycinthium-lapis lamp buzzed uncontrollably, before failing completely.

"Protests will not bring your son home, Alan. If anything, they will put him at risk. Where will the men focus their frustration when they're missing the white cliffs of Cadbey?" said Arthur, as Alan exhaled in concern. "You may have a seat at the king's table, but you're not the vice admiral anymore. You must let go. I'll do the heavy lifting."

Alan had awarded his position to vice admiral Oswald Leonard. Oswald was a spirited, well-respected man of great cunning. He was eccentric and relentless. He had always been three steps ahead of friend and foe. But Alan had not heard from him in months.

"Aye, I suppose you're right," said Alan. "But I can't forget what they did... I will never forgive them for that."

Agitated, Todd burst into the kitchen, where Arthur and Alan were seated at a dining table.

His father was an elderly gentleman who reeked of tobacco. The smell was imbedded in his flesh. The brass buttons, of a beige vest-jacket, glinted in the sunlight cast from a window. Sun beams exposed how thin his white, slicked-back hair had become, but his handlebar moustache remained lustrous. Alan had rolled his sleeves up; a habit that preceded any debate. Both arms resembled manuscripts of scars. Weathered tattoos had become relics on his skin, ruined by warfare. Even his large hands were caked in calluses, and his muscles had solidified making him strong with age. His grey eyes harboured nightmares, his face was a map of the world, and every etching harnessed a story.

Arthur's appearance was the opposite, despite them being of a similar age. He was tall, slim, and clean shaven. His body had not been weathered because his life had been soaked in luxury. Only time had faded the colour of his shoulder length hair. A velvet tailcoat lined his figure. Jewelled fingers held a matching top hat. Despite their differences in wealth, Alan and Arthur had remained friends since primary school.

"Why do you hate the Skuas!?" Todd blurted. Only Arthur jumped from his skin as the minion appeared.

"Why're ya not at school?" Alan replied. Todd was staggered by his father's calmness. He stopped to think.

"Mr Lilly is sick, so our maths class was cancelled." Arthur raised an eyebrow in suspicion, but Alan was too proud to accuse his son of truancy in front of a friend.

"Well, there's nothin' ya can learn in school that ya can't learn from king's council. You'll have ta accompany me and Arthur ta the palace. You're not stayin' here, Witherow junior." Todd gasped as they rose to their feet like titans; chairs scraping along the tiled floor.

"I don't think the king's table is any place for a child," Arthur muttered, placing his hat on his head.

"Nonsense… consider it work experience for the lad." Alan grabbed a long, double breasted, naval coat from a peg beside the grandfather clock. Its buttons and medals had been polished to perfection. Each one brandished the Skua emblem. Excited, Todd made for the front door, when his dad's hand clasped his shoulder. Alan's palm dwarfed his frame.

"Todd, accuse me of hating the Skuas again… and I'll have you guttin' fish for a week in the trawl yards. Is that clear?" said Alan. His son gulped and nodded before they departed.

Chapter 2
The Table of
King Oborus

Todd, Alan, and Arthur cut through a vibrant market plaza. A fisherman shooed a cat from stealing his take, sparks rocketed from a blacksmith's hammer, and herbalists proclaimed their potions to be miracles. Further stalls and caravans could be found in the shadow of Cadbey's cathedral. Todd felt dizzy when he looked up to admire its enormous towers and spires. Divine monuments and incredible sea beasts swarmed its marble exterior. A gargantuan, bronze door told the story of Allód: a great prophet who had come from overseas to deliver the word of God. Hooded priests patrolled its entrance like ants, lecturing the desperate and needy, whilst others preached from balconies.

"God is the one true protector. Let him into your heart," an elder wailed from beneath his burgundy cowl. "Let faith be your shield, abandon your sin." A shiver ran down Todd's spine as their eyes connected. He struggled to believe their stories, and many monks seemed intimidating.

To Arthur's concern, the church's influence was spreading. The priests sought reform, but their fanatic visions would not bring prosperity. They believed hycinthium-lapis should be left in the ground, due to its unnatural properties. And they felt the Skuas could be replaced with missionaries, boasting the word of God.

Todd was towed down a crooked alley, where lopsided dwellings overhung a cobbled street. An old woman, hunched and bitter, poked Arthur's chest.

"Tell those toffs to leave us be. We're happy as we are, thank you very much!" Bemused, the minister continued his journey. Todd asked his dad why the woman had intervened, but Arthur answered.

"These people have become blinded by fear. They fail to see that if we don't start moving people outside the walls, we'll have another pandemic on our hands," Arthur boomed, as if he were practicing his speech for the table of King Oborus. Talk of a resettlement programme had besieged the ancient settlement. But its reasons remained unclear.

"What are they afraid of?" Todd asked, as they exited onto a downward street. An experimental, road-going steam-engine screeched uphill, spewing smoke into the air.

"A distance from God," Arthur shouted. "The cathedral has become a second home for many whose faith in God has increased, whilst their faith in the monarchy has diminished." The Skuas were no longer favoured due to their growing brutality, roaming factions had long dented Cadbey's dominion over Arcaya, and gluttonous lords blamed the king for their peoples' suffering.

"Not that our shores have ever been breached," said Alan with pride. People's attire improved as they entered the business district. Wide streets gave way to more arachnid drones, steam engines, and couples enjoying alfresco dining. Suddenly, a child waved a newspaper in their faces.

"Skua raid successful! Sundrithia subdued!" Seconds later, another paperboy approached them with a different headline.

"Demand the truth, 'Sundrithian farmers murdered!'" A passer-by snatched the paper and threw it at the floor. The boy's employer abandoned his stall, stormed across the road, and grabbed the man by his collar! Todd thought his father might intervene, but they could not delay the king.

The king's palace stood as both an icon of convention and progression. Granite columns stemmed from a megalithic bed of marble. They framed shimmering, stained-glassed windows, and the sculptures of heroes and monarchs, who kept watch over its walls. Todd's lungs were burning by the time they reached Isabella's Square: a large plaza that lay before the political temple. Its foundations were immersed in history, for they contained deep dungeons and colossal catacombs. King Harold's conquest of Arcaya, in the late fifteenth century, had convinced him to convert the old castle into a palace. This inspired a renaissance, but some feudal features still remained, such as the turrets abreast its roof, and the ancient tombs below its splendour.

"Come on, lad we shan't be late," said Alan. His son had paused, whilst climbing a mountain of white steps. Alan came to a merciful stop at its peak. Todd felt as if he had traversed the mountains of Terra province.

"Remember, Todd, we're in the company of the king. The most powerful people in all the land come here ta shape the world. You're here ta listen, and ta learn, is that understood?" The statue of an R.B.S marine seemed to scowl at Todd, but he nodded in excitement. A sturdy hand patted him on the back. Then, they entered the beating heart of Cadbey.

An atmosphere of eminence engulfed them. Many professionals greeted them, as they swept through a grand hall dotted with elegant pillars. Portraits observed their journey, as their footsteps echoed in the distance. Sunshine fell from a skylight high above a twin stairway. Its steps curved around a beautiful statue of Queen Isabella, so she could be admired from all sides.

Isabella was nineteen years old when her father, King Harold died, leaving her the throne. Many had detested the idea of a female monarch, but her advisors were adamant she would succeed. After all, it was her father who had united Arcaya. So, Cadbey turned its sights to the Aeternum Ocean, and a growing Merithian presence. The R.B.S was formed in

28

1538 under a mother's reign, resulting in countless military victories. Resolute, Isabella had overseen the final construction of Cadbey Cathedral and Zora's Lighthouse in the late 1500s. She finally died in 1601, after guiding the kingdom into the seventeenth century.

The stairway took them to the king's hall, where the council had gathered. Alan guided Todd through a doorway packed with ministers. He tightened his grip on his son, as they had to wait until the king had been seated. A central table stretched towards a throne cast from igneous rock. Its varnish reflected the ceiling, where endless brush strokes had created a map of islands, swirling sea beasts, and famous ships. Todd gawped, as he tried to absorb its brilliance. Hycinthium-lapis chandeliers cast a crimson glow. Their constant illuminance was a sight to behold. A far door opened resulting in silence. King Richard Oborus III and his advisors emerged. They marched past the spoils of war, which decorated the granite chamber. Todd squinted, so he could study the king's appearance.

Oborus was twenty-eight years old and twelve years into his reign. His jet-black hair had been stylishly ruffled, and bristles defined his slender jaw. Smooth cheekbones, and soft lips, corresponded with his gentle, cobalt eyes. The king was yet to take a bride, but he was handsome, and time was on his side. A red sash appeared bold against his black, military tunic. Polished buttons, and a gold trim, lined the pelisse jacket, which had been fastened around his slim figure. Matching trousers brandished the same finery.

Unexpectedly, it was Oborus's advisors who stole Todd's attention. Purple cowls and brass masks hid their faces, which belonged in the catacombs far below their feet. Their robes swept the floor. These solitary figures kept their identities hidden by residing in the palace, where they were safe from conspiracy. Only those most devoted to the monarch would be promoted to the role of advisor. Todd found their appearance and secrecy unsettling.

"All be seated," an advisor shouted. A symphony of chairs erupted. Todd awkwardly positioned himself beside his father, who was seated near the end.

The advisor continued, "The council have hereby been summoned to discuss… required funds for the restoration of saint Woolford's Pier; required funds for the expansion of the industrial sector; required funds for the restoration of Cadbey Cathedral's eastern spire; the resettlement of market district civilians to Red Rock Citadel[9]; Winsford's law, first born enlistment to his majesty's boat service, and an enquiry into the Sundrith raids." The councillors became uneasy. Todd leant forward so he could see their faces. As expected, Admiral Alfred Sartorius and General Ernest Bestla were present. They were seated beside the king as his ceremonial hands. The left hand was responsible for the navy, and the right hand was responsible for the army, otherwise known as the Oborian Guard. He did not care to recognise the other lords and ladies. But paralysis set in when he realised Mr Ackerley was sat opposite! His frown had persevered, and it did not lessen when he spotted Todd. Arthur inadvertently saved the boy by springing to his feet.

"Though it's not first on the agenda, I would like to discuss the resettlement of market district civilians to Red Rock Citadel." The king nodded in approval. "I know the honourable, Lord Ross and the honourable, Professor Langley Stewart will support me in declaring hycinthium-lapis vital to the growth of Cadbey's prosperity. In just eight years, eight years ladies and gentlemen, the properties of this stone, and Langley's research and brilliance, have brought light into our homes." Arthur raised their attention to the chandeliers. "They've provided heating systems that can cast out winter. They've produced marvellous machines that can transport

---

[9] Red Rock Citadel is the capital of Arca province, run by Lord Whitmore.

heavy goods. We have skimmer boats; red rock[10] propulsion engines that will see our galleons replaced with iron ships. The possibilities of this gem seem endless, yet there's *still* so much we can learn. Ladies and gentlemen, this precious resource, and Langley's mind, will alter the course of humanity as we know it." His audience nodded in agreement and waved their papers, which Todd found odd and amusing. Langley glanced at Mr Ackerley and his counterparts.

Lord Ross was responsible for the industrial sector. His plump stomach had absorbed a large chunk of his wealth, but he desired more. Rosy cheeks matched the heat of his workshops, and his cold eyes resembled lumps of coal. His monocle reflected the crimson glow of a new age.

"However, we still lack the infrastructure and the workforce required to mine red rock," said Arthur. "I believe Lord Whitmore has the latest figures." Wilfred Whitmore coughed to clear his gullet. He slowly unravelled a scroll across the table. Then, his trembling hand plucked a magnifying glass from his pocket. Arthur sighed with impatience.

Lord Whitmore ran Red Rock Citadel and its infamous mining colonies. Red Rock Citadel existed in the heart of Arca[11] province, where the streets were paved with gold. Most of the gold had been excavated, but pockets of hycinthium-lapis were being discovered daily. This ore was yet to be found anywhere else in the world. However, these pockets existed in Terra province, deep within the mines of Vanth and Nadym, otherwise known as Dead Man's Chasm[12]. Only the imprisoned or damned were sent to toil in such dangerous conditions. The Oborian Guard could not protect Arca, Terra,

---

[10] Red rock is a common term used to describe hycinthium-lapis due to its colour or crimson glow.

[11] A wealthy mining province in western Arcaya.

[12] The mines of Vanth and Nadym form the Southeastern corner of Dead Man's Chasm, where hycinthium-lapis is found. Both are run by Lord Whitmore and his Crimson Guard.

and man its prison mines, so Whitmore had enlisted his own army, the Russam Guard. Named after the Russam Mountains surrounding Red Rock Citadel, his soldiers had been dubbed the Crimson Guard due to the colour of their uniforms.

"Last month's survey concludes that six new dig sites, established in Vanth, are running at an eighteen percent capacity," Whitmore chuntered. A hooded man whispered in the king's ear.

"That's a ten percent drop since last time we spoke. Explain," said Oborus. Whitmore looked to his peers for support, like a pig stuck in the mud. But it was General Ernest Bestla who provided an answer.

Bestla's attire was not dissimilar from his majesty's, except for a black bicorn hat that shadowed his cratered face. An exotic feather, a military heirloom, pierced the air and drew attention from his skin. Acne and battle scars created the illusion of a curse upon his flesh. This veteran of steel was responsible for the Oborian Guard, as well as law and order. Lords begged him for security. Others implored him to look away. War was in his blood.

"The mines have come under regular attack from tribes your highness. As you know, Terra is not a province we can easily hold due to its arctic conditions and barbarian hordes. Such conditions have made it difficult to mobilize troops, many of which I've lost due to rapid expansion and a sudden demand for protection from settlers." Bestla placed his glare on Whitmore. Arthur felt he was losing the crowd, so he coughed abruptly before speaking.

"This is why we need immediate enhancements in infrastructure, relocation, and security. Thus, I propose a one-billion-pound investment, to fully obtain and utilize red rock." Arthur staggered when he noticed another advisor muttering in the king's ear.

"How have my people taken to the idea of relocation?" Oborus asked. He disliked the idea of resettling his people in an unstable province, much to the frustration of his ministers, his lords, and their monopolies.

Arthur stuttered, "In good nature. The people fear a pandemic due to overcrowding, which must be seen to." High Priest Howard Healy interrupted Arthur's drivel.

Healy wore a deep red robe. Its cowl warmed the back of his neck. Whisps of hair circled his rumpled head, and a long white beard covered his front. Healy's gentle voice and wide, sapphire eyes emphasized his godly wisdom. Todd fell victim to his tones.

"I beg to differ," said Healy. "There's limited concern of a pandemic your highness. The cathedral provides healing and ensures a good standard of self-preservation for all. Especially for those residing in the market district, who have chosen to live under the wing of God." Todd knew the priest was correct. Healy had exposed Arthur's ploy, and he proceeded by damning red rock. "Such a stone is unnatural. It holds too much power for any man to wield. It should be kept in the ground from whence it came," Healy urged, which caused Professor Langley to scoff. Many desired red rock for their own ambitions. The church was considered delusional for wanting to ignore it. "Our children suffer. Many are forced to pick up arms and join the Skuas or the Oborian Guard. Those who stay struggle to breathe the air, whilst their fathers feed the furnaces, or work the mines. Do we really wish to see an expansion of this industry? Are the Skuas not brutal enough without this unholy stone to power their murderous ships? It's not God's will."

"Was it not God who put it there?" Langley mumbled, which caused his peers to snigger. To Todd's amazement, the king's left hand, Admiral Sartorius decided to speak.

"As long as Merithia poses a threat, our brutality will know no bounds… but the high priest has spoken some sense for a change. No one fears a pandemic your majesty. And besides, this is going against tradition."

His skin and sanity had been worn by the sea. His appearance, however, was well kept. A crafted, silk beard reached his navy jacket. Gold epaulettes matched his medals, and the buttons on his cuffs. A metallic eye patch glinted, as Sartorius shuffled in his chair. This brass cover, another medal of sorts, seemed fused to his skull. His handlebar moustache brushed its edge. Sartorius often seemed distant or troubled by his blood-stained past.

"This isn't about tradition," Arthur replied. "This is about ensuring Cadbey's future. The future of humankind."

"Need I remind you; I have three thousand of the king's personal guard at sea, providing for Cadbey's prosperity," said Sartorius. He was referring to the Royal Skuas, who were considered the king's personal guard.

"Here we go again," Professor Langley muttered.

"Marines who've always provided for Cadbey's prosperity. I suppose you wish to reduce the navy's budget *again,* to fund your northern gallivants?" Arthur curled his lips. "Campaigns that've only ever ended in disaster. Six times we've tried to conquer Terra province and six times we've failed, which is why we've always returned to the sea. We should draw the border at Arca and be done with it."

"We haven't failed under my watch," Bestla stated arrogantly. He had not been tasked with such a doomed military endeavour. Previous commanders, including his great grandfather, George Bestla II, had succumbed to the ice, never to be seen again.

"Blasted red rock or not, all that lies north is tundra and death," Sartorius concluded.

"And death is all that lies to the south thanks to your recusants!" Mr Ackerley shouted. He had not forgotten Todd's presence. "Is it not time we discussed the legality of recent Skua raids along Sundrith's shores, and the reports, which claim a hundred civilians have been left homeless or face down in the dirt?" Lord Whitmore, Lord Ross, and Professor Langley all jeered in agreement.

Ackerley had been appointed as the minister for education. This new role required liberal thinking, but Ackerley's goals were radical. Some suspected him of being a republican. Many feared the rise of left-wing politics, driven by intellectuals and the working class. Their movement was growing, and no one could be sure who was involved.

"You mean the same raids that have kept a growing threat at bay, whilst adding millions to the king's treasury? The same raids that will pay for Woolford's Pier, industrial expansion, and your bastard spire?" Sartorius revealed his false hand, by jabbing it at his colleagues. Most of him remained lost at sea.

"Fingers in your ears, lad," Alan told his son. These debates often boiled over, and Mr Ackerley was frothing.

"Your highness, times aren't changing, they have *already* changed. The industrial revolution demands that these dissenters not only be dropped from the curriculum but be disbanded!"

"Reformed!" Alan intervened. The council fell silent in respect. "Honourable sailors still bleed ta keep these shores safe, so you can sleep soundly in your beds, no longer haunted by our enemies, who still strive ta see these lands in ashes. But it's true. The Skuas no longer represent the Cadbey I stand for. Their ranks must be challenged."

"Why don't you go and sit with them blundering fools!" Sartorius blasted, so Ackerley continued his attack.

"The Skuas are too far gone. Reform cannot cleanse the corruption or make amends for the dead," said Mr Ackerley. "Sir Witherow's calls for reformation simply confirm that the unit should be disbanded!"

"The finance *is* needed elsewhere," Whitmore mumbled with Langley and Ross in support. Sartorius growled in resentment.

"The treasury is robust and there's enough finance for all," Arthur confirmed from a standing position. The lights coincidentally flickered above their heads. "However, if we can press ahead. There would be an economic benefit to scrapping Winsford's law."

Winsford's law was fundamental to the kingdom. It stated that, 'the first born of any standing Royal Skua must serve in the R.B.S.' Many civilians and veterans, including Alan, wished to see this law abolished. It had been weaponized by the republicans; it had driven a wedge between the monarchy and its people, but Sartorius detested by banging his fist against the table.

"Does nobody care about tradition anymore? The Skuas are a family. It's what makes them tick. How can you suggest such an idea?" Todd cringed, as Sartorius spat, "You don't surprise me Arthur, but Alan... I expected better from a night devil."

"Do *not* speak those words," Alan replied. "I'll not be known as a night devil. Those words shame what was once an honourable unit." Many felt uncomfortable, except for Bestla, who loved to see the navy squabble.

"Is it not treasonous to suggest such things," Bestla suggested, before turning to face the king. "After all, the Skuas are your personal guard, and there're those who wish to see your guard... diminished, your majesty."

Royal power had slowly been dissolved into a semi-constitutional monarchy. The third Oborian era had brought further dissolution, but several lords desired an oligarchy, and unquestionable power.

"Is that an accusation Bestla?" Alan asked, though Bestla was more concerned about the lords to his left. Alan's toes curled in rage. "I've given everything for this kingdom: my blood, my wife, my eldest son serves as we speak. How dare you suggest treason!" Todd knew nothing about his mother's fate, only that she had died when he was young. But his heart skipped a beat when he thought of Thomas, fighting on the high seas.

"Disband the unit your highness," said Mr Ackerley. "Let us be done with glorified pirates assaulting the possessions of foreign dignitaries."

Sartorius jumped to his feet and yelled, "Maybe you should propose the idea to Vice Admiral Leonard and Commander Grenyard when my marines next come ashore, you gutless pig!"

"Maybe I will, you putrid bastard!" Mr Ackerley rocketed to his feet, as if to engage in a duel. Although Oswald Leonard was well respected, Ackerley feared the thought of Grenyard. Alan was beginning to regret Todd's presence, yet the boy had gained a valuable insight. Then, Mr Ackerley switched targets.

"As for you, Sir Witherow, I shall be enquiring why your boy isn't in school, and why he's been attacking students in the playground," he said, as a method of diversion. Alan looked confused, before realising his son had deceived him.

A war horn blasted through the chamber! All fell silent. Even the king raised his head in alarm, as if Cadbey was under attack. A second horn reverberated through the great hall, signalling the return of the Royal Skuas. A guard burst through the door and delivered a formal announcement.

"The Royal Skuas have returned!"

Sartorius relaxed his shoulders and shouted, "Come then, Mr Ackerley. Let's go propose your idea shall we!?" Ackerley swallowed a bitter pill. His attention was no longer on Todd's absence from school. But Alan's focus was.

"It seems you've got some explaining ta do, boy," said Alan, as Sartorius marched past.

"Status report?" the admiral requested. He was impatient to learn why the Skuas had returned.

"The ship looks to be in good condition. Only one casualty," said the guard. A lengthy bayonet matched the height of his shako[13].

---

[13] A tall cylindrical military cap.

"They've already docked... what sort of operation are you running here, Bestla?" Sartorius gunned. The horns were supposed to sound once the mothership had been spotted on the horizon.

"Says the admiral who knows not why the mothership has returned," Bestla replied. Sartorius smiled arrogantly before leaving.

"One casualty," Todd muttered. Alan became sympathetic, as Todd expressed a look of concern.

"Don't worry, lad. I'm sure your brother's fine. Let's head home."

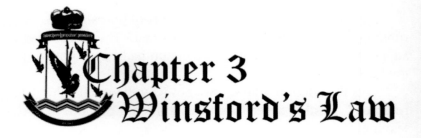

Chapter 3
Winsford's Law

Jared spat his drink overboard and cursed in revulsion.

"Tastes like horse piss," he shouted, as their skimmer boat jumped a duo of waves.

Sodden, his torn trench coat thrashed behind him. The gauntlets around his gloves had rusted. Knee-high boots strained to keep him upright. Yet, a shredded bicorn hat stayed glued to his head.

"It's all that's left," Ness yelled over the engine. "You can see the King's Mouth; once we're through you can have whatever takes your fancy."

Her sopping, bloodred hair flicked in the wind, and her petite nose matched its colour. She had one foot on the gunnel, which allowed her boot buckles to glisten. Leather gloves grasped the support ropes around her. She kept her back against the cabin. A dripping poncho covered her slight frame. Vanessa Griffiths, known as Ness, was usually quiet, but a long journey from Thindraka to Cadbey had agitated her.

"Don't worry, Jared. I hear those harbour girls taste sweet enough, ain't that right, Spike?" Robert shouted. He was seated on a notched bench at the stern where Jared was stood.

"I'd leave the harlots for Grenyard and his dogs if I were you. Besides, I'm overdue a pint with my Pa," said Jared. But he glanced at Ness, whose emerald eyes returned a wanting stare. Their comments were designed to hide their romance. Winsford's law meant it was illegal for marines to become entwined.

Jared Kader's scarred buzz-cut, violet eyes, and bronze skin originated from Sundrith. His father, Laith had fled the deserts for the shores of Arcaya with his remaining son. The ocean had made him strong, and fearless, but the twenty-five-year-old sapper[14] had much to learn.

"Well, I'll at least take that grog off your hands!" said Robert. Jared staggered towards him, so he could snatch the bottle.

Robert Simpson was known to his friends as Simmo or Rob. Blue eyes revealed a caring soul, nineteen years of age. Yet, many had died at the end of his revolver. Bullets swilled around his boots. Their mother, a mounted Gatling gun, slumbered nearby. The mechanical turret mirrored Rob's size and stature. He had always been cumbersome, despite spending years at sea, which is why his poncho looked more like a tent. The gunner's beard hid his neck, and cropped hair formed a jagged formation on his head. Enthused, he turned his attention back towards Spike. She had barely spoken a word since leaving the mothership.

"Thank you - by the way," he shouted. Spike bobbed inside a battered cockpit, as if she were possessed. Wooden beams, peppered in bullets, groaned around jingling equipment. Her silence persisted, so Rob continued. "...For taking us in. I couldn't stand to come ashore with Grenyard, or the crew... especially in these circumstances." Rob was referring to the loss of their captain, Thomas Witherow, and the disappearance of vice admiral, Sir Oswald Leonard.

Spike stayed silent. The side of her head had been shaved, to reveal the tattoo of a sea-beast, which arched around her pierced ear. Its long teeth grazed her snapped eyebrow, and its tail slid around her neck. Bolts of blonde hair ran down the other side of her trench coat. Braids escaped her bicorn hat, which loomed over the wheel like a beak. Her crystal eyes displayed beauty. But they were shadowed in charcoal, which

---

[14] A combat engineer or demolitions expert.

bled down her cheeks. And the onyx thorns on her shoulder pads, and the bullring in her nose, made onlookers think twice before approaching her. Like a viper, she was ominous, quick, and satanically ruthless. The nails protruding from her uniform had earned her the nickname, Spike.

They approached Cadbey's white cliffs. Cathedral spires stood above a fortress wall, where stone sentinels loomed over their approach. Seabirds swarmed the godly spears. Then, their vessel soared towards the King's Mouth. Its gate remained sunk amidst an arm of stone. An echo thundered off its archway, causing a few guards to peer down in confusion. Spike's skimmer burst into the harbour like a cannonball, where she fought to dodge approaching ships.

"Ease down!" Rob shouted through the salt spray. Awestruck, Jared and Ness observed Cadbey's beauty, and its colossal bay.

"Makes it all worthwhile, doesn't it," said Ness. The fractured façades of the cape stretched to their left. Uneven walls and turrets lined its narrow edges. Only the cathedral had risen above the stronghold. Everything was bathed in gold, for the sun had begun its descent. The mothership had moored beside the largest dock: Woolford's Pier. The immense galleon dwarfed any other ship in the bay. Its sails beat; a collage of black and white Skua emblems. To their right, Zora's lighthouse was burning bright in the eyes of homesick sailors. It towered over the bay like a second sun, fixed in the sky. Finally, their boat reached a jetty wrapped in seaweed, where its engine fell silent. They could finally hear townsfolk going about their business, the lapping of waves, the squawking of seabirds, and the screech of a train in the distance. They were home.

An old man came hurtling towards them, as fast as his boiler suit would allow him.

He shouted, "Pray that my eyes do not deceive me, Eleanor is that you!?" Tony Archer went to embrace his daughter, Spike. She shunted him away.

"I forget her name's Eleanor," Rob sniggered.

"Leave it, Simmo," Jared ordered.

Spike detested her father as much as her real name. He claimed her mother was a whore, who had chosen to lay with strangers in exchange for coin. Sadly, the rumours were true. But it was Tony's anger, abuse and alcoholism that had driven her away. Spike was three years old when her mum disappeared, never to be seen again. Yet, she could still remember her mother's cries and the beatings that would follow. And she could still remember the smell of liquor, and monstrous visits in the night, when all was black. Spike had joined the Skuas immediately, so she could leave Cadbey far behind. A bloated stomach connected Tony's hunched shoulders, withered arms, and rigid legs. The tattoos on his scalp had faded. Missing teeth, broken blood vessels, and sore eyes signalled his time was limited.

"Let me know what needs doing to your ship. But first, let's have a drink. Where's that apprentice of mine? Edwin, bring up five beverages from the store! Edwin!?" They began unloading their equipment, as a small boy in an oversized flat cap delivered the goods. Spike spotted the child's bruises, before eyeballing her father.

"How long has it been? Eight, nine, ten months?" Tony pestered.

Jared interrupted, "Tony, listen up. The headlamps are knackered and the hythe[15] is nearly snuffed. The cabin's on its last legs. Oh, and port side contains more holes then an Arca brothel. Once you've fixed those, I'll let you know what else is wrong with her."

"It'll cost ya," came a stern voice. They looked over to see Tony's boss, a skinny man in overhauls. His crooked jaw revolved around a toothpick, whilst the wind lifted his comb over. "And those beers as well."

"They'll pay," Tony insisted.

---

[15] Slang for red rock or hycinthium-lapis.

"In full," said the creep.

"What about our discount?" said Spike. "What about our deal…"

"Your terms have been revoked. My dock, my rules. If you don't like it, you can piss off… Don't you know there's a revolution coming?" The man disappeared. The Skuas became frustrated. But Spike did not flinch. She would convince Tony's boss to change his mind if he valued his flesh.

Only a few engineers knew how to maintain skimmer boats. They were revolutionary machines from a far-off era; one of Langley's creations, inspired by the marvels of red rock. To Spike's disapproval, they had no choice but to rely on Tony's services. Reeling, the marines grabbed their gear and headed along the harbour. Seabirds swooped and squawked, as droplets fell from copper clouds. Jared came to a stop. A large crowd had gathered around the mothership.

"I thought we were giving the celebrations a miss?" said Rob.

They listened for a while, until Jared replied, "That's no celebration." Robert, Spike and Ness followed him down Woolford's Pier, and into the midst of an angry mob. Rotten fish and tools spiralled through the air, as they tried to separate the masses.

"Murderers!" someone cried.

"Heroes!" another screamed. The crowd were fighting amongst themselves. Spike yelled, as an elbow struck her right eye. She instantly slammed the culprit to the ground. Triggered, another protestor threw a punch. Robert stepped forth, caught his fist, and nutted their foe unconscious. The protestor's nostrils spewed blood, as they collapsed into a stack of barrels. Further rioters approached the encircled sailors, who shoved the crowd in desperation. A cannon bellowed! Everyone ducked. Only the Skuas remained standing, as the warning shot struck a wave in the distance.

Then, Commander Grenyard snarled from the mothership, "The next shot will be at your feet!" Grenyard's volume, severity and stillness were frightening. "Allow us to unload the dead, otherwise you'll be joining them!" Jared could see his scars, all the way from the pier. A cursed wind rustled his gothic attire. His sword reflected a dying sun. Withered hair grazed an eye patch, framed by tampered flesh. Two sailors carried a stretcher down onto the pier. The body of Thomas Witherow was upon it, wrapped in blankets.

"We should be carrying him," Jared admitted, but their presence would reveal the body's identity. Ness placed her hand upon his shoulder and swallowed her pain.

"What the hell's happened whilst we've been away?" Robert asked. The calls for a revolution were growing. Arcaya's inhabitants were falling out of love with the monarchy, and its conventional protectors.

Spike smeared her swollen eye and said, "Move, now."

Grenyard's eye observed the defenceless, as Lieutenant James Crawford appeared beside him. Crawford's demeanour was just as fierce, but he lacked mettle and battle's mark. Still, he resembled a fine sailor. Crawford kept his face shaven and his attire pristine. Grey hairs had snaked their way through his side parting, which he would often rearrange, before replacing his hat.

"Look at them... cowering like dogs. You can tell they've never heard a cannon fired in angst," said Crawford, his tone eloquent and educated.

"It's time that changed," Grenyard demanded.

***

Todd shivered before scrambling into bed. A lamp fuzzed beside him, and toy boats cast shadows across his room. The floorboards creaked, as Alan entered. He had kicked off his boots, unfastened his vest jacket, and the day had unravelled his moustache. He sat on the edge of the bed, before raising an eyebrow at his son.

"What?" Todd asked.

"Normally I can't get ya ta shut up come bedtime. Yet, I take ya ta see the king, and I don't hear a peep?" Exhausted, Todd mustered a question.

"Do the council always argue?" Alan chuckled and nodded. "Why?"

"Too much testosterone… not enough women to make the men behave… and probably too much of this." Alan swished his nightcap - a whisky.

"Why did Arthur lie about the lady in the street? He said we should relocate to stop getting ill, but all he talked about was people going to work in the mines," Todd questioned. Alan sighed, but he had encouraged the boy.

"Sometimes, the council have ta do what's best for the kingdom, rather then what's best for a small number of people. For example, you hate going ta school. If it wasn't for me, ya probably wouldn't go at all. But if ya don't go ta school, you'll end up shovellin' horse muck for the rest of ya days. So, in the end, you'll thank me for it," Alan explained, before taking a sip.

"Except for today," Todd grinned.

"Aye, well you'll not pull that stunt again, if ya know what's good for ya," said Alan. "What's this about you attackin' other kids in the playground?"

"It was Spindler. He deserved it. He was calling Tom, and the Skuas, and he slapped my book out of my hand!" Todd explained, as if his tongue might catch fire.

"Aye, I thought as much," said Alan. "Where did you hit him?" Todd hesitated before admitting, 'In the crotch,' which caused his father to laugh. "Don't worry about Mr Ackerley. I'll deal with him. But try and keep yourself out of trouble, lad."

"Was mum a councillor?" Todd asked.

"No, but she certainly kept me in check. What makes you ask that?"

"You mentioned her today."

"Aye, that I did," said Alan. He could never bring himself to mention Todd's mother, and the truth about her origin. The veteran grimaced when he realised Bestla had provoked him.

"The world is run by selfish men, who don't care ta understand what's beyond their doorstep. Don't believe the history they've written. Don't grow up to be like them. You're better than that. Make your own decisions," said Alan.

"How do you know I'm better?" Todd asked.

"Because you're my son. And you've got your mother's brains. And her locks. It's about time we got you down the barbers." A large hand ruffled Todd's hair.

"Do you think Tom was on the mothership?" Todd asked. Tom's bed remained undisturbed on the opposite side of the room. His favourite books and treats awaited him.

"Well, he's not here is he. But we'll find out soon enough, lad. Anyway, off ta bed with ya. It's been a long day."

"If he's home, will you take us to the theatre, to see the new puppet show?"

"Let's see what your brother says, eh?"

"Or kite flying?"

"Todd, bed." His son retreated beneath his blanket, so Alan switched the lamp off. "Good lad. Sleep tight," he said before quitting Todd's room.

***

A thunderous knock caused Todd to jolt from his bed. The sun cast beams through his window, which revealed a ballroom of dust. He gasped, as another knock caused his possessions to rattle.

"Mr Witherow open the door!" Todd raced to his bedroom window. A flock of naval hats had besieged their house.

"Hold your horses, I'm coming!" Alan shouted, as he struggled to put his boots on. Open buttons revealed his scarred chest. Still, he opened the door to Lieutenant Crawford. The officer looked down his nose at Alan, before asking if they could enter.

"Suppose I say no?" said Alan. He led them into the kitchen. Crawford took a seat opposite the veteran. Alan could tell this was not a social call. He counted six Skuas.

"Where's my boy?" said Alan.

Crawford paused before replying, "Your son is dead. He died valiantly serving his kingdom." Time stopped. Alan clenched his fists.

"How did he really die?" he asked.

"Serving his kingdo-"

"Details man!" Alan barked. His chair scraped in alarm.

"He was shot following a raid," Crawford muttered. He feared Alan's fury. His reputation was not unknown to the lieutenant.

"Where?"

"A Sundrithian fort," said Crawford.

"So, he died for no reason."

"He died bettering his kingdom," Crawford argued. Todd peered through the banister, as if he were a prisoner in his own home. Tears welled in his eyes. He could barely see Crawford, who was sat beyond a mob of trench coats.

"Protecting his kingdom? He died as part of an illegal raid. Since when did a Sundrithian ship ever skirt these shores?" Alan shouted.

"They were amassing a navy," said Robert. He pushed his way into the kitchen. His eyes were sore, he had been up all-night drinking, but he had to intervene. He knew Alan, and Thomas had always spoken highly of his father. "I was with him the night he perished. There was nothing we could do. He died a brave man and a fine captain." His blue eyes begged for calm.

"Interrupt me again, and I'll have Grenyard cut out your tongue," said Crawford. Rob retreated towards the doorway, where he sensed a presence. He looked up to see Todd, perched on a step, smearing his nose with his pyjama sleeve. The sailor discreetly signalled him to leave, but Todd had frozen in misery.

"Your son will be buried three days from now. Then we depart, which means I must move swiftly onto our next topic. As charted in Winsford's law, your remaining son is to serve in Tom's place, so I shall be leaving with the boy," said Crawford.

"You come 'ere, ta tell me my son is dead. And expect to leave with my youngest!"

"It's the law, Mr Witherow," Crawford replied. The air grew thick. Again, Rob signalled Todd to leave, but the child remained still.

"The boy is ten years old! Ya have ta be at least thirteen before ya can serve the king!" said Alan.

"I'm aware of no such clause," Crawford lied. "You will reveal the boy to me, and we shall be on our way." Pride assured him that his authority was absolute. He was mistaken.

"Like hell I will," Alan yelled, before slamming Crawford's head against the table. Cutlery bolted, as Crawford's men rushed the veteran. Pulsing with wrath, Alan uppercut a sailor and nutted another, but the troopers overwhelmed him.

"Go!" Rob told Todd through gritted teeth. Horrified, Todd sprinted downstairs and out the front door.

"After him!" Crawford shouted, before blinking and smearing blood from his shattered nose. Then, he rose to his feet. Alan had been restrained on the floor like a wounded lion.

"We'll find your boy a position mopping decks! No one will ever know his name. As for you, your name will rot in a dungeon for defying Winford's law and attacking the king's personal guard. Take him away!" Crawford ordered, so Alan unleashed a torrent of abuse.

Todd dashed along Hadley's Road. Tears blurred his vision, as people stopped to observe his distress. Then an arm swept him off his bare feet! Todd struggled, as his captor bundled him into an alleyway. It was the homeless veteran Todd had spoken to on his way home from school. A woollen tea-cosy warmed his head, and his beard tilted in the breeze.

"You're ok, lad, I don't mean no harm. I saw those Skuas storm your house, and I knew it was nothin' good!" The old man stopped the boy from hyperventilating. "Take a breath... good, that's it... now what just happened?"

"They said my brother is dead... and they arrested my dad."

"Young Tom... You have my grievances, lad. And Sir Witherow has been arrested. That is bad news." They both mourned for a second. The beggar said, "Listen closely. I swore to serve your father a long time ago. And I've been keeping watch ever since."

"What's your name?" Todd asked.

"You can call me Eldrid. Now, I take it those Skuas are looking for you. The best thing you can do is go to them. I know you don't want to, but there're good men and women who will look after you. It beats being on the streets, or in some orphanage, take it from me," said Eldrid. Winsford's law could not be defied. A shiver ran down Todd's spine. Their shelter was hidden from the sunrise, whereas the cathedral was blessed in rays. Rats scurried past in alarm, like commuters on their way to work.

"Don't worry about your old man or the house. I'll keep an eye on things, and I'll see to it that your father is ok. I promise you that." Todd recoiled in dread, as a Skua appeared in the alleyway. It was Rob, but Todd was not sure how to react. The large sailor raised his hands in peace.

"Todd, isn't it?" Rob asked. "It's ok. I served with your brother. I'm not going to hurt you." He took a moment to assess the situation, and catch his breath, before dropping to one knee. "Lieutenant Crawford is looking for you. If you stick with me, I'll make sure you're assigned to our unit. I'll keep you safe. It's what your brother would have wanted. I owe him that much." Todd looked at Eldrid who nodded in agreement.

"You served with my brother?" Todd asked.

"Go on, lad. Your destiny awaits," said Eldrid.

Todd was returned home, just as Crawford was leaving. His father had already been escorted away.

"Lieutenant, I've found him. He was hiding a few streets from here," said Rob.

"Congratulations," said Crawford. "As a reward, the boy is your responsibility. Do with him as you please." The lieutenant left them standing in the street, so he could tend to his fractured nose.

Rob nudged his new companion and said, "See, it's already going to plan." But Todd was cold and distraught. "Come on, let's get you some clothes." He prayed for his father, before taking one last look at his home, in the shadow of Hadley's turret.

Chapter 4
The Swoop

An obsidian cane sent shockwaves down the stone corridor, as Grenyard approached the office of Admiral Sartorius. Lamps winced at his presence. A guard clasped his rifle.

"Bullets don't hurt me boy," Grenyard shouted. He came face to face with the guard, who shuddered at the sight of altered flesh. Grenyard removed his eye patch, to reveal a soulless organ. It had been seared by the inconceivable, a sight no human eye should see. A bellow asked who it was, the guard answered, and Sartorius appeared.

"Remind me, Admiral. How does it feel to be guarded by spineless virgins?" Sartorius sighed and invited Grenyard in. Fine art, drapes and taxidermy covered the bricks of a lonely room. A log fire roared beneath a cast iron chimney. Pelts smothered its oak floor. Sartorius took a seat behind his desk, where bookshelves formed a backdrop. Relics from a past life dotted his chamber: maps, model boats and nautical apparatus. His false hand slept on the desk beside him, so he placed a whisky decanter under his arm before opening it.

"Is it done?" Sartorius asked.

"Yes, Admiral. Witherow reacted the way we anticipated. He's rotting in a cell and his life is in your… hand," Grenyard answered.

"Good, that will put a stop to his ranting about reforms," said Sartorius. Grenyard's ghostlike stare was unbreakable, so Sartorius filled two tumblers with whisky, but his commander refused to partake in a drink designed to honour the man they had imprisoned.

"I have another assignment for you," Sartorius declared.

"With all due respect, I've not come ashore to hunt old men and left-wing scum. Have you considered my request for the position of vice admiral?" The chimney howled, which caused the fire to spit and crackle.

"No, commander. It's been less than a day since you reported Vice Admiral Leonard missing."

"Dead," said Grenyard.

"A body hasn't been recovered, and no one saw a thing… He's missing." Sartorius could not understand Oswald's disappearance, and he would not be intimidated by Grenyard, even if the man stood before him like a corpse possessed. The Skuas had returned to report the absence of a great leader. Grenyard had returned solely to replace him. Oswald's status remained confidential.

"I appreciate the R.B.S needs a vice admiral, especially in these treacherous times. We can't show any bleedin' weakness… The seas call you back. Complete this assignment and I'll consider your promotion." Sartorius pulled a scroll from his draw and handed it to Grenyard.

"Who shall I bring death upon?"

"Your first mission is the same as before. Find Johnathan Ackerley. Have your men threaten or provoke the bastard," Sartorius commanded. "He's the minister for education, and the headmaster of Cadbey Academy, but he's become a thorn in our side. He's the cornerstone of a movement to have us disbanded. He's turning the whole damn system against us, as well as the next generation of little bastards," Sartorius explained.

"Consider it done," said Grenyard. Sartorius handed him another scroll.

"Here's your second target. Send your dog Rias. Kill him."

***

Ness awoke and took a deep breath. Her emerald eyes observed a familiar ceiling, but she could not feel the motion of waves. To her relief, she was home. A gentle breeze caressed her skin. But a weight lay heavy on her chest. Ness gasped when she realised it was Jared's arm. A vile hangover struck her brain as she sat up, causing him to stir.

"God, I wish I was dead," Jared murmured, as the light stung his eyes.

"You have no idea how lucky you are," Ness replied in a husky voice. She noticed his toned physique and broad shoulders, as Jared took a moment to remember his whereabouts.

"Did we-"

"No," Ness interrupted. "But you should still consider yourself lucky." Jared sighed, as she pulled a blouse down over her body. Scarlet hair draped her slender back. The dawn radiated her beauty, but Jared could only complain.

"They say the quiet ones are the worst, but months at sea, a night in your bed and we still haven't-"

"Don't blame me," said Ness. "I'm not the reason you missed your chance. And don't go blaming Winsford neither." She smiled at Jared's drunken demise, before wriggling into a pair of pantalets. Then she positioned herself beside the window.

"Go on then, off you go," she commanded. Jared huffed and gathered his possessions. After all, this was her parent's home. Ness was barely twenty and Jared was six years older. Her mother, Niamh, a fiery Skua veteran, would kill him if she caught him.

"See me tonight," he suggested, before giving her a lasting kiss.

"Since you asked nicely," she replied.

Jared landed on the cobbles below, before trekking through a maze of snickets and streets. Birds soared overhead, the thaw glistened, and the moon remained in a magenta sky. A few oil lanterns had nurtured their flames throughout the night. These beacons prevented shadows from gathering under lopsided houses and slanted steeples.

"Who's a dirty stop out then?" Spike asked. She was stood, legs crossed, arms folded, against a cast iron fence. A shredded, bicorn hat hid her face, but Jared recognised her gruff voice. "Don't think I don't know where you've been." She puffed on her smoking pipe.

"Jealous?" he asked without stopping. Spike exhaled a stream of smoke and joined his march like an alley cat.

"You two were exchanging looks all night. I thought I was gonna retch. Grenyard will have your heads if he finds out," she replied, for Jared and Ness had broken Winsford's law. "I'm here to keep an eye on my squad."

Jared faced Spike and said, "*Your* squad. Since when?" He fought to keep his voice down. No one had been promoted since Tom's death - their team was leaderless.

Spike's crystal eyes contained the oceans. Smudged charcoal covered her crow's feet, and a nose ring distracted his vision. Typically, her right eye was bruised from the riot on Woolford's Pier. Blonde hair evaded the thorns on her shoulder pad.

"Come on, Jared. You're a fine sapper, but you couldn't tie your bootlaces if it wasn't for me," said Spike. Jared turned away, to avoid her stare and the smell of tobacco. Alcohol choked his mind.

"None of us are safe. Half the city wants us dead."

"Dead?" Jared replied. "Don't be daft."

"The calls have gone beyond disbandment. Whilst you were raiding Ness, I was hunting down rioters." They started walking again. Jared was too arrogant to believe her. The Skuas were heroes. "It's all about the red rock now. Bestla's losing his grip on the provinces, the lords grow restless, and a revolution is brewing."

"And does that mean Cadbey has found new ways to protect itself?" Jared asked. He spotted a carrier drone in the distance, which had come to a standstill in the cold.

"The people have gone soft. They don't believe the seas pose a threat," said Spike. The brass arachnid was covered in ice. Its tormented faces had petrified in the night.

"Do they think machines or red rock will save them?" said Jared. "My Pa helps build these. He reckons they'll man the turrets someday... but the red rock soon burns out. Just like in our skimmers."

"Is that the same Pa you were overdue a pint with?" Spike said sarcastically. "Let's keep moving. We're meeting Simmo at The Swoop. Lieutenant Crawford pulled him from last night's events. I want to know why."

"The Swoop's not open yet."

"They'll open it for me."

It was barely midday, but The Swoop Inn was bustling. Despite this, Jared became a husk, as his hangover took hold. Spike slammed her tankard down to keep him awake. She had missed this loyal nest of filth and debauchery. Drinkers, gamblers, harlots, merchants, and veterans could be heard in every corner. An aroma of tobacco, sweat and ale had conquered the tavern. A veil of smoke had degraded every surface. Candle wax had dried on the brick work, beside placards and portraits. Beer matts, brandishing the Skua logo, had been pinned to beams and booths, where clandestine figures discussed new endeavours. Red rock lamps cast a crimson glow across their stern faces.

"Where's Rob, and where the hell is my steak?" Spike shouted. A grizzly landlord assured her it was coming. He sweltered behind a bar that looked more like a barricade.

"Tell me, is the loin for that shiner you've gained, Miss Archer?" the landlord asked. He was referring to Spike's black eye. Jared cowered from the light shining through a block window behind her.

"How can you sit there with a pint?" he asked.

"Get a grip," she replied, as a plate of overcooked meat invaded their table.

"And how am I supposed to know where Simmo is. You're the one who arranged this excuse for a piss up. But if Crawford's got him running errands, he might not even show," said Jared. But Spike spotted their gunner through the crowd.

"Speak of the devil," she muttered. Robert ducked several beams to reach them. A strange boy followed closely behind, who was dressed in his brother's oversized, hand-me-downs.

"Sorry I'm late," he grumbled. "Flippin' heck, Spike. How can you sit there with a pint after last night's antics?"

"That's exactly what I said," Jared murmured. Spike questioned who the boy was.

"Meet the youngest and latest member of our squad, Todd Witherow," said Rob. He hoped his team would approve. Spike stopped chewing.

Jared lifted his head and mumbled, "You takin' the piss?"

"Lieutenant's orders, under Winsford's law. The boy's sibling is no more, so he must take his place... Sorry, Todd," Rob explained.

Jared became animated and said, "Hang on a second. You can't just dump a kid with a bunch of sea dogs like us. What the hell are we supposed to do with him?"

"I don't know," said Rob. "I don't usually go around nabbing kids under Winsford's law!" His comment attracted the attention of pub dwellers.

"Let's take a second," Spike suggested. She dropped her cutlery and smeared her mouth. She knew Winsford's law could not be defied, even if the people deemed it unjust. "How old are you?"

"Twelve," said Todd assertively. Rob mouthed the number, 'Ten'. Jared shook his head in disbelief.

"And where's your parent?" Spike asked.

"My mother died when I was young... and my dad's been arrested..." Spike acknowledged the boy's strength. Todd was done sobbing; his dad had taught him never to cry in front of others.

Bewildered, Jared lent forward and whispered, "What if he ends up like his brother?" Spike placed her lips beside his ear, so Todd could not see or hear.

"Forget that. Have you not listened to anything I've said? The people will have our heads if they think we're carrying a ten-year-old boy off to war."

"Is that why you've brought us to a pub, where we're surrounded by people?" he replied. Spike sat back. She believed there was no place safer than The Swoop. They were surrounded by the finest ex-servicemen and women in Cadbey. Rob could sense the tension was rising.

"I'm gonna get me and Todd some pork scratchings," he suggested, before shepherding the boy away. Jared denied his hangover by gulping Spike's ale. She questioned what choice they had against Winsford's law.

"We leave him," said Jared.

"You n' Ness might be in the habit of breaking Winsford's code... Leaving him could get him killed, and us," Spike stated, before reclaiming her tankard. Todd could be charged with cowardice and the boy was Robert's responsibility.

"He doesn't stand a chance at sea... we leave him here before anyone knows he's a part of our squad. His father will take care of him, or the orphanage, or someone," Jared concluded.

Ness appeared and asked, "So, what have I missed?"

***

Arthur hurried down a dank passage of foreboding shadows. A key ring jingled, as the minister demanded haste from his escort. They eventually reached Alan's cell, where Arthur told the guard to disappear. He stood before the bars of an alcove, barely big enough to stand in. Alan looked undignified in striped rags. Brown arrows marked him a possession of the crown.

"Alan what in God's name-"

"Don't start," Alan replied. "You expect I'd let them take my only blood?" A meagre flame revealed his confines, where a ball and chain kept him grounded. Putrid blankets offered little comfort.

"You have my greatest sympathies regarding Thomas... but you attacked the king's personal guard. That's treason. I don't have to tell you this," said Arthur.

"Like I said, don't start. So, how're we gettin' out of here?"

"Alan... there'll have your neck for this. I fear the Skuas are mounting an aggressive campaign, against a public desire to see them abolished."

"That doesn't answer my question," said Alan. His candle fought for oxygen, so Arthur answered.

"I'll speak with Sartorius, the advisory, and the king if I must. I'll get you a position working the mines."

"I'd rather die!"

"Don't be so stubborn," Arthur barked. "I'm not making you a part of my policies. I'm trying to save your life!" Arthur stepped forth, so he could speak between the bars. He whispered, "You still have friends who would risk their lives to help you. These dungeons are impenetrable. The mines are not so solid." Arthur was referring to Eldrid and a group of former Skuas, who had sworn an oath to protect their commander, as well as the kingdom.

"And who'll be looking after my son?" Arthur was Todd's legal guardian. He would try and save the boy, though Winsford's law could not be easily overruled. The guard confirmed their time was up.

"God be with you," Arthur prayed.

"We both know God won't get me out of this mess," Alan complained, so Arthur turned to leave. "Arthur," Alan pleaded. "...Good luck. And thank you, old friend." Arthur nodded in respect before leaving.

***

Todd's new guardians stumbled from The Swoop Inn, as a carrier drone scuttled past. Cobbles and manure broke beneath its feet, and drunkards fought to dodge its path. Storm clouds had arrived from afar to ruin the sunset. Ness helped Spike onto the street, as Todd took refuge in Robert's shadow.

"Jared, give me a hand," Ness demanded, as Spike sang in praise of her favourite tavern. A lustrous bard followed, whilst fiddling a tune.

"Night devil's they call us, night devil's they say,
for we swoop when the shadows present us with prey,
but we're devils post dawn, aye we're devils by day,
so we drink in the swoop where your daughters do stray!"

"Can you piss off, please?" said Ness. Disappointed, the bard stopped and disappeared inside. Jared placed his arm around Spike, to help her stand up straight. Prostitutes circled them like vultures, desperate to escape the rain.

"Same again, Miss Archer?" a harlot asked. She wore a black corset and a frilled dress. A velvet mask covered her eyes, and a bowed brooch was tied around her neck.

"So, this is the new example we're to follow?" Jared asked. He was sleep deprived and Todd's presence frustrated him.

A blast shook the ground! A sobering fear heightened their senses. Then, a bloated wall of smoke approached them. Grit fell from the sky and screams wailed in the distance, as panic poisoned the city. People began fleeing in all directions.

"On me, now!" Spike ordered. Robert insisted that Todd stay behind him. A shiver ran down the boy's spine. This was to be his first duty as a Royal Skua.

Their squad tore downhill towards the explosion. They passed singed victims, who fled the blast. Jared lurched, as a black stallion galloped past. Then, their eyes fell upon a scene of carnage. An overpass had collapsed between two decimated houses. Flames roared, pulsing smoke into the air. Viscera lay strewn across the street. A smouldering wagon lay beside a charred horse, and its contents lay burning on the ground. Screams gripped them, as a family pleaded to be released from their terraced house. Rob and Jared raced towards a cordon of rubble. Roof tiles crashed beside them, as they hurled brick from the doorway, until the family could squeeze to safety.

"God bless you," a mother cried, as she hurried her children away. Robert blessed the rains, for there was nothing more they could do. Meanwhile, Spike recovered a bicorn hat from the rubble. Skuas were amongst the dead. She looked towards the sky in anger, and let the rain sober her. Eventually, Cadbey's soldiers arrived to confront the howling flames. They questioned what had happened, as a steam engine delivered water, men, and hoses. Giant red wheels supported its tank and pumps, but the weather did more to kill the fire's fury. Rainfall revealed an inverted grave of blackened memories. They approached the wreckage, and glowing embers scattered like rubies, to investigate what remained. Ness spotted a carrier drone. One contorted face remained on its burst body.

"Look, its metal has splintered outwards. The blast came from within," she confirmed.

"That's the same drone that passed us at The Swoop just now. Maybe it was supposed to stop there?" said Jared.

"And it could be the drone we saw at dawn," Spike suggested. It was odd to see a drone outside the industrial sector, left to the merciless dawn.

"There could be more of these things out there waiting to explode," Rob shouted. Spike summoned the nearest commander. Mutton chops escaped his military cap, and his blue tunic championed medals of gold. She ordered him to seize every drone in the city. The Skuas held rank, as the king's personal guard, so the trooper obeyed. Todd shuddered in grief. He had lost himself in the abyss of a dilated pupil, belonging to the lifeless steed. Robert put his arm around the boy, to protect his vision. Cadbey's walls had withstood siege. Its people had rioted in the streets. But it had never experienced an attack of this nature. Jared questioned their next step.

"We need strength in numbers. Let's head for the barracks, double time," said Spike.

The Skuas made their way towards R.B.S headquarters, situated near the harbour. Todd had always wanted to visit the home of his heroes. But his stomach turned, as they approached beneath thunder. Black pillars, fierce emblems, and spiked fences lined its perimeter. Gargoyles surrounded its apex roof. Sandbags were being stacked six-feet high. Ness questioned if they were at civil war.

"State your business!" a Skua demanded through the downpour.

"What do you see!?" Spike shouted. She pointed at her uniform, and the thorns on her shoulder pad.

They entered a hall reminiscent of a museum. Skua emblems draped its high walls and balconies. The granite floor reflected a hive of crimson lamps.

Todd gazed up at a skimmer boat. It had been suspended beneath skylights as a centre piece. The light reflected off its ironwood[16] body, which was approximately twelve meters long and five meters wide. Retired Gatling guns peered over its bow and stern. Todd admired its revolutionary propellors and rotors. Then, he spotted its heart: a steam powered red rock propulsion engine. Its pipes and brass components were visible, just beyond its dissected hull. This marvellous contraption had rendered the skimmer's sail obsolete. A central cockpit and cabin housed its wheel, nautical instruments, a cast iron throttle, and two benches either side, used for work or sleeping. A fortified boiler stood in front of

[16] Ironwood or lignum vitae is the strongest wood known to humankind.

the cockpit. Three, sloping, iron sheets surrounded the container, and a vault door faced the bow, which could be loaded with coal. This metallic structure also contained a superheater, boosted by hycinthium-lapis elements, capable of producing rapid superheated steam. Exhaust pipes stemmed from this fortification, around the sides of the cabin, before splintering off into the air. A central pipe carried steam around and down through the cabin, to its L.H.L.M[17] engine. Valves lined the iron artery, beside gauges and bolts. A hatch lay between the cabin and the stern, where a hycinthium-lapis battery could be lowered into its depths. Steam powered boats, carrying iron and fire, had been deemed too dangerous for civilian use. But Langley's hybrid motor would change everything, and the Skuas had been the first to test it.

Lieutenant Crawford was amongst the crowd. His sweat smothered brow spelled trouble. He had just finished briefing a monster known as Rias Lyman, Grenyard's closest and most feared captain.

Rias was short for Zacharias. The sinister being wore a tampered top hat, which often concealed his glare. It would occasionally lift to reveal piercing, unnatural, arctic eyes. His cropped beard failed to hide a satanic scar on his left cheek. His moustache looked like a formation of pikes. Rias was no taller than Jared, but his shoulders were broad, his chest was wide, and his arms could crush bone. His navy-blue, double-breasted coat swayed, as he stopped beside Spike.

"Little sparrow... come to hide from the storm," he muttered. His haunting voice lacked emotion, as did his stare. Spike despised the nickname Rias had given her. It was designed to dilute her venomous bite. Jared's eyes were drawn to a fishhook, clenched in Rias's gloved hand. Its silver was elegant but deadly.

"Going fishing?" Jared asked.

---

[17] Langley's Hycinthium-Lapis Motor invented by Professor Langley Stewart.

"Yes…You could say that…" Rias replied. He awaited a response, but none came, so he exited the hallway.

"Prick," Spike muttered. She collared Lieutenant Crawford before he could escape. His clothes were soaking and wretched, and a dressing covered his broken nose.

"What are we supposed to do with this?" she demanded, before grabbing Todd by the arm. The boy stumbled to her side. Crawford looked resentful, so Todd mirrored his glare. He could not stand Spike's demeanour or appearance. Her nose ring offended him, as did the spikes on her uniform. Yet, their individuality set them apart as an elite unit.

"As discussed with your gunner, the boy is your responsibility. Put him with the cadets. Then reside in the barracks and remain on standby. Any leave has been revoked under martial… law." Crawford's attention was stolen by General Ernest Bestla. His feathered hat cut through the crowd like a periscope and his cape shed the storm. Bestla refused to extend his hand.

Instead, he stabbed the floor with his cane and said, "Lieutenant Crawford, I bless your halls with my presence since you've not bothered to set foot in mine. I understand Admiral Sartorius is somewhere amongst this relic. Take me to him if you'd be so kind." The officers departed upstairs, so Rob insisted he would show Todd to his barracks.

They disappeared down a corridor, aligned with naval portraits, where further lamps provided a crimson glow. The ten-year-old said their names aloud, which impressed his guardian. After a brief history lesson, they reached the cadets' sleeping quarters. Blue doors concealed a rabble of cubs.

"Time to make some friends. Remember, Todd, you're not just representing the Witherow line. You're representing our squad. Don't forget that. Oh, and if anyone asks, you're a part of Sabre Squadron, just like your father and brother before you, got it?" Rob signalled the boy inside. "Go on, you can't sleep out here." The cadet gulped before entering a narrow room, lined with beds. Oil lamps revealed twenty, maybe thirty imps amongst the darkness. Ancient brickwork had been chalked in blue, Skua emblems had been stencilled in white, and bedside chests bore the etchings of souls long gone.

"Who're you!?" A teenage girl approached with haste. Todd was stunned by her aggressive, candle lit beauty.

She positioned herself before him and placed her hands on her hips. A light blue shirt draped her skinny figure. White hair flowed off her shoulders, like the glacier falls of Silvashire[18]. Freckles dotted her nose, and a beauty spot complemented her left eye, which differed in colour from her right.

"Oh my god, what are you wearing?" she laughed, which caused the other children to snigger. For a moment, Todd was back in the playground. He looked down at his brother's hand-me-downs: an oversized coat, gaping boots, and baggy trousers.

"My name is Todd Witherow," he declared. The girl paused.

"Witherow... as in the old vice admiral's youngest son?" Todd nodded in apprehension at her mesmerising smile, and wide, gorgeous eyes. "Oh my god your dad is a legend... as was your brother."

"What do you know about my brother?" The girl paused and thought, as a quiet respect infiltrated the group.

"He was kind... caring... funny... yet still hard as nails."

"I heard he died, during a raid... Is that true?" said Todd.

She nodded and replied, "We were below deck when it happened... He was the finest captain this unit has ever seen." Todd dipped his head in acceptance. "Allow me to introduce myself. I'm Carla Bennet, Foil Squadron." She curtsied in a playful manner.

"Are you part of Sabre Squadron?" another girl asked him.

---

[18] The Kingdom of Cape Cadbey's most northern province, ruled by Lord Walter McQuillan. A province blessed with stunning highlands.

Her name was Abbey Shelton. She looked younger than Carla, but older than Todd. She was sat cross-legged on her bed, under a large blanket. Platted brown hair framed her face, and a gap in her toothy smile. Her blue eyes were innocent and gentle. They stole attention from her fragile frame. Abbey took an instant liking to Todd.

"Of course he's a Sabre," Carla replied in a profound voice. "A sabre is a quick sword that takes the enemy by surprise!" In a flash, she grabbed her dagger from a bedside trunk, and began stabbing the air. Her feet skidded as she pranced across the tiles. Todd's face lit up.

"Calm it down, Carla," Gregory moaned. "We're in lockdown and your pissin' about isn't helping."

He was sat on his bed; hidden amongst the gloom. A pudding bowl haircut ran parallel to his monobrow, and his rosy cheeks had become flustered.

"Shut up, Gregory," said Carla. She stabbed a folded shirt from his bed. Abbey repeated her command like a parrot, before giggling in amusement. Gregory's whining prevailed, so Carla flung it at his face.

"In case you're wondering, that's Gregors. Delightful fellow. As are all those in flatulence squad."

"Falchion Squadron," Gregory shouted. Todd knew that all Skua squadrons were named after swords. But the name Sabre had become legendary thanks to his brother, father, ancestors, and the brave marines who had served them.

"Alright, don't get mardy," Carla muttered before regaining her breath. "So, welcome to the family, Todd. I'd head to the back and change if I were you." Abbey jumped off her bed and hurried towards him. She was taller then Todd, but a tough upbringing had rendered her skinny.

"My name's Abbey. I'm in Rapier Squadron... You can have the bed next to me. No one's slept in it and there's a uniform on it you can have," she insisted. Todd thanked her with a simple nod. He remained composed, even though he was overcome with kindness. Finally, he could rest, in the comfort of friends.

***

Night had engulfed the city. A heavy downpour pounded Rias, as he prowled the docklands. He was not fazed by the bitter sting of rain, but his target was. Despite the curfew, a man quit The Earl's Corner Club by the cellar door, and hurried home. The social club had become a redoubt for republicans. Rias recognised his target and knew which path he would take. A shadow, Rias dashed down an alley, slid between a fence, and clasped his victim by the neck! Ackerley choked, as he was dragged into the blackness.

"You thought this day wouldn't come. You thought there'd never be a devil waiting in the shadows, but you've played with fire, and now the fire burns," said Rias in his haunting voice. He nudged his hostage towards the harbour. The bay glistened beyond the end of a narrow passage. Rats shrieked amongst the filth, whilst avoiding their boots. The storm had cooked up a smell of disease and rot. "You thought you could stop us with your clever drones... yes... I lost good men today!"

Rias tightened his grip, as Ackerley croaked, "That wasn't us!" But Rias was blood thirsty, and his time was short.

"Liar," he groaned, as they reached the end of the passage. The opening was hidden by looming structures. "I've been ordered not to kill you," Rias admitted. "But you are the enemy, as proven today by your bombs, and you know what we do to our enemies!" He removed Ackerley's gullet with his fishhook. Blood gushed from his throat, as the headmaster gurgled for air. "We... *are*... the realm," Rias whispered. A gentle push sent Ackerley plunging into the waters below. The heavens growled, and Rias watched in hatred, as the minister slipped beneath the murky waves. Then, the malevolent marine set off in search of his next target.

***

Bestla entered the admiral's office as if it were his own, but he felt as if he had stepped into another dimension. Sartorius had created a cavern, reminiscent of a sunken ship. Thunder tumbled down a large chimney breast, as if a demon were gaining entry. Crawford, Bestla's escort, awaited the que to stay or leave.

"Piss off, lieutenant," Sartorius ordered. The officer swallowed his pride and left, closing the door behind him. A strategic silence followed.

"I'm not offering you a drink, Bestla. Wine's a harlot's tipple and you can't hack navy liquor!"

"That's because it's made of piss," said Bestla. He took a seat. "Besides, now is not the time for games."

Sartorius laughed, "Now's the *perfect* time for games. You've put us in lockdown!" The admiral unplugged a cork and poured a shot of vodka. His brass eye patch reflected the flames that riled Bestla's back. The general unbuttoned his coat and threw his cape aside. A sabre remained belted to his hip.

"As the right hand, I would urge you to remain sober," Bestla insisted. The tactician despised alcoholism.

"And I would urge you to sod off. Yet here you are, like a thorn, firmly wedged in my side," said Sartorius. Bestla's personality was dry and sinister. Sartorius, however, was temperamental and quick to react.

"I know you only care for matters at sea, but need I remind you, you're ultimately responsible for the king's safety, and since your sailors are ashore, you're obliged to participate in his protection." Sartorius grumbled and shot his drink.

"Don't patronise me. I already have people on the case." Concern crept across the general's face. He questioned what Sartorius meant, but the admiral refused to say.

"So, you're aware the drones came from inside the palace grounds? Since they bear the royal insignia. Whoever armed those machines had access to the palace," said Bestla. "So, who do you suspect? Using drones as bombs is unheard of. A Merithian wouldn't know their way around a drone. Rebels? Republicans? The church?"

"You forgot one," said Sartorius. "The Oborian Guard." Bestla laughed half-heartedly at the accusation. An awkward silence followed, which preceded fear. The general expected an assassin to appear from the shadows. His sabre beckoned his fingertips. But no such threat emerged.

"You think *I* want the throne?" Bestla asked. Sartorius did not react. Bestla silently questioned the state of his sanity, before asking, "Where's Oswald?" The vice admiral had spent years building bridges between the army and the navy, yet he was nowhere to be seen.

"He's none of your concern. Oswald has ongoing business at sea," Sartorius lied.

"The mothership returns without its vice admiral. That's unheard off." Bestla's inquisition only served to annoy his counterpart. "This is getting us nowhere." Frustration caused him to up and leave, but Bestla turned before departing. "My forces will be interrogating suspects and checking drones throughout the night. Should no further attacks take place, I will lift the lockdown. In the meantime, why don't you investigate your own ranks, instead of questioning mine. The Skuas also have access to the palace."

Chapter 5
The Merithian

Todd's breath lingered before him. Nothing could pierce the fog, except for the ash that fell and settled on him. Then, the cobbles beneath his feet began to vibrate. Fear gripped him, as the thunder birthed a wild stallion. The beast raged towards him; wide eyes bulging with madness! Hooves collided with his body!

Todd screamed as a pillow slammed his face. A barrage of laughter followed. The shellshocked cadet took a moment to remember where he was. His toy boats had disappeared, along with his brother's bed, and the sun had yet to rise.

"You scream like a soddin' girl," said the attacker. Neal Finley tossed the weapon aside. The prankster was unnervingly tall and thin, and fanned hair added a few more inches to his height. Bushy eyebrows stole attention from his gaunt features, and acne. He was already dressed in his uniform: a black linen shirt, shorts, and tattered, buckled shoes that longed for death.

Abbey sat up in bed and shouted, "Leave him alone!"

"You were tossing and turning and snoring like a pig. Be thankful you didn't get whacked you mut!" Neal replied.

"Pick on someone your own size, Fin," Carla insisted from her bed on the other side of the room. Todd became calm. Carla's beauty prevailed, even at dawn. She wiped the sleep from her eyes and puffed hair from her mouth.

"I wouldn't wanna disturb ya. You need all the beauty sleep you can get. Grenyard will be strappin' ya to the bow of his ship to scare off Merithia," Neal joked. Gregory laughed from beneath his blanket. He opened his hair like a pair of curtains, to reveal Carla's glare. DUMPH, DUMPH, DUMPH - a knock at the door triggered a drumroll of feet! Todd followed in alarm.

"Good morning, all! No need to salute, it's only me." The cadets became deflated as Mr Sweeney entered the room, but Todd's spirits lifted. "Since your commanders are a little preoccupied, I thought I'd come and find you myself." Sweeney's moustache had overshot his top lip. The same dusty, tweed-suit sheathed his nimble frame. But his eyes lit up when he spotted Todd. Then he remembered the tragic circumstances surrounding his presence, and the older brother he had once taught.

"My sincerest apologies regarding your brother. I can only imagine what you must be going through." Todd remained silent, so Sweeney continued. "Still, it's an honour and a privilege to have another true sabre amongst our ranks. You're probably wondering why I'm here. I teach common folk during the day and you young whippersnappers at dusk and dawn, when you're ashore that is. Hectic? Yes. In which case, we don't have much time, and you'll probably be off to sea in a few days, so if you wouldn't mind joining me in the classroom that would be superb!" Sweeney's busy schedule explained his appearance, and Todd realised why headmaster, Johnathan Ackerley was so distasteful of his employee. Ackerley despised the Skuas, yet Sweeney was responsible for the next generation of cadets.

Abbey helped Todd find his uniform. He dived into a black linen shirt, shorts, and a pair of buckled shoes. Next, he placed a navy neckerchief over his head. He tightened it using a woggle displaying the Skua emblem. Then, they hurried through the main hall, where the skimmer boat was suspended. Sweeney awaited them in a cold classroom. Portraits observed their frosted breath as they entered. A chalk board covered the far wall, like a portal to unseen lands. Plaques explained the Skua emblem, maps showed the far reaches of the known world, flags deciphered friend from foe. Lamps revealed a model skeleton, beside a miniature skimmer. Weapon racks, props, and other mock-ups had been pushed aside, and blanketed in cobwebs. Sweeney ordered everyone to take their seats.

"For those of you who're new, if you're expecting to learn about poetry, think again. These lessons are designed for one reason and for one reason only: to keep you alive. You'll only get a few hours of my time, so listen carefully. I'll then assign you a task to be completed at sea, which will be marked upon your return-"

"If we return," Neal blurted. Sweeney repeated his comment in agreement. Abbey gave Todd a concerned look. Even Carla's enthusiasm faltered, for the risk of death was certain. Sweeney's chalk stick went to work. *'Lesson One: know your enemy.'* Bouncing, he asked who their sworn enemy was.

Gregory cried, "Merithia!"

"Wrong! Your sworn enemy is nature," Sweeney declared. "We already know all there's to know about Merithia. A Merithian may even spare your life. But nature... she's a cruel beast."

The hours that followed were gruelling. Sweeney covered every topic possible. Constellations became familiar guides. Myths became fact. Todd learned about fearsome creatures, such as the Horned Scolopendra. This horrifying, human sized centipede would lay eggs in its dying prey. Then there was the Insulor Consumptor: a mass of tentacles capable of suffocating entire islands. This titanic beast had been dismissed as fantasy, but the Skuas had seen it, and they dare not cross its path. Further creatures would gift them shivers in the night. Large portions of the world remained unchartered, especially in the Ocean of Väldiga[19], where alien creations

---

[19] A desolate, unchartered ocean framed by the western shores of Sundrith and the eastern shores of Scavana.

dwelled. The great explorer, Wilbert O'Hara had determined the globe was somewhere between 70,000 and 80,000 kilometres in circumference, but many parts of the jigsaw were missing.

A lesson in basic first aid followed. Abbey partnered with Todd. They practiced dressing pretend wounds made from chicken bones and gristle. But Todd was obsessed with Carla, who scoffed at Gregory, and his lame attempts at applying a bandage.

"Greggory, if we're on a boat, and I get injured, promise you'll just shoot me."

Abbey grabbed Todd's fingers and stressed, "Please pay attention, Todd… if one of us gets hurt, we need to know how to save each other's lives." There was fear in her voice, so Todd regained his focus. Then, they were shown how to kill.

"This isn't a game," Sweeney stated. "If your mate is in peril, then you need to know where to strike; hard and fast. Meet Beryl!" Sweeney grabbed the model skeleton by the hand and pulled it into the spotlight. "Beryl didn't *listen* during class, meaning Beryl didn't *know* how to protect himself or his mates. Beryl is now *dead*!" A few children laughed, whereas Abbey remained afraid. Todd was still struggling to comprehend Sweeney's presence.

"Imagine you're small, timid, and weak. No stretch of the imagination there. Now imagine Beryl is on your captain's back. Beryl's murderous, ravenous, jealous! He knows he should have paid more attention in class. What do you do?"

"Shoot him," Todd answered.

"And risk shooting your captain!? Besides, the recoil would tear your arm off," said Sweeney.

"Kick him up the arse," Neal joked. Sweeney revealed a Skua dagger, which caused the arrogant teenager to sit back in his chair.

"No, Mr Finley. I suggest you take your royal issue dagger and stick it through Beryl's armpit!" Their teacher lifted the skeleton's arm and thrust his knife between its ribs! Cobwebs fled the scene. "This attack should avoid any armour, pierce the heart, and kill your foe. Understood?" The children tried to grasp such an act and how they could ever be so callous. Todd tried to picture Rob, Ness, Jared or even Spike in trouble. He decided he would have to do what was necessary, to protect his crew. But he had never experienced war, death, or humanity's searing brutality.

"What if we don't have a dagger?" Abbey asked with beaming blue eyes.

Sweeney replied, "In that case, Miss Shelton try kicking them up the arse." A few children laughed, as Sweeney made his way over to a draw. "You will each be issued a dagger. Your mentors, however, will be armed with something that came from Sundrith."

"Ha, what have Sundrithians ever invented?" Neal questioned.

"This." Sweeney turned and pointed a revolver at the teenager, who nearly fell out of his chair! "It's not loaded you burk!" Sweeney declared, so Neal could regain himself.

"That's not funny," he grumbled, as the others sniggered.

"You're right, Mr Finley it's not. This is a Tait Mathieson revolver, which has only just been patented. Most think it's years ahead of its time, but it wasn't dreamt up by Tait, or Mathieson, or Langley for that matter. The original design comes from Western Sundrith, as did gunpowder." The cadets observed its smooth grooves, floral patterns, and the carving of a skua on its handgrip, as Sweeney span its revolving cylinder. "Far superior to any musket; more accurate and no more reloading after each shot. And a bastard to manufacture; these have only been issued to the Skuas and officers, for now."

"Can I hold it?" Todd asked.

"One day, Mr Witherow. I'm sure you will."

***

Rias swept through the upper reaches of Cadbey Cathedral. His footsteps echoed off elegant sculptures, and a chequered floor dashed in sunbeams. Yet, he felt encouraged to stop and admire the view. He had witnessed it once before, as an orphan, decades ago. Shortly after, he had been expelled from the church, to be raised by the Skuas. Now he had returned, to punish those who had forced the word of God upon him. A chill ruffled his beard and crooked top hat.

Slate-grey clouds covered the horizon. They bled into a darkened moor, where a morning dew covered the land. A jigsaw of houses lay below, which led all the way up to the palace. He could see the business district and its wealthy houses; the industrial sector and its smog infested railway station, which lay beyond the citadel walls. He remembered inquisitions about his origin. He remembered refusing to conform. And he remembered physical torture. Suddenly, a monstrous skua landed in his window. Rias did not flinch, as the seabird screeched a deathly command.

"All in good time," Rias replied. Implored, he removed a vial from his pocket. He opened the capsule and emptied its contents. A tainted breeze, from a distant realm, carried a stream of blackened salt towards his prey. Guided by an unseen hand, Rias continued in search of his second target, High Priest Howard Healy. The bird watched in glee. Eventually, Rias reached a medieval door and entered without permission.

"Can I help you?" an elderly priest barked from the foot of his bed. He had just finished putting on a burgundy robe. Rias scanned his surroundings. This was no longer the chamber of a pious man. Gold twinkled atop fine furniture, luxurious fruits sustained the wicked, a lady of the night loitered beyond a lavatory door. The harlot appeared and complimented Rias's appearance, but he would not be distracted by her naked flesh.

"Oh dear," Rias droned, for he would have to kill her as well.

"What business does a vile night devil have with a priest?" the priest growled.

"What business does a priest have with a whore?" Rias replied. "Wait… I know you." Fear gripped the elder. He recognised Rias's arctic eyes. But the Skua was a far cry from the orphan he had abused and abandoned. The harlot approached.

"Are you one of Larry's men?" she asked in a fluster. "The priest pays well, and he treats me kind. Larry can find someone else to gobble the butcher's mea-" Rias slid a Merithian knife from his sleeve and launched it at the woman. The projectile punctured her eye socket, then her body smacked the floor. The priest tried to scream, but terror blocked his throat. Rias remembered his name.

"Father Halbert Smythe. Yet what father abandons his son," Rias boomed, as he stepped towards his former guardian. His eyes pierced his soul. "Too long have you spoken heresy against us, the true protectors of this realm. Too long have you sought power through lies. Too long have you convinced the people to feed off false hope, whilst we bleed to provide." Smythe's tongue was thwarted, so Rias continued in his haunting voice, "No more preaching. No more lies. It's time to pay for your sins." Then he thrust Smythe with a second Merithian dagger, several times, until his struggle became weak. But Rias was not done. "You used to place my head on the alter and cane my tongue for questioning your false God. Yes, you remember," Rias droned. As Smythe lay dying, Rias cracked open his jaw, pulled out his tongue, and cut it from his throat. Mutilated, his victim writhed. The silk sheets became bloodied, as scarlet pools expanded across the chequered floor. Finally, Smythe stopped moving. "You saw a darkness in me. You should have known that darkness would return…" Satisfied, Rias placed a fictitious note written in Merithian. Then, he discarded Smythe's tongue alongside the Merithian blade, before leaving.

Perhaps the people would restore their faith in the Royal Skuas, now their beloved church had falsely been attacked by Merithia. Regardless, the Skuas had sent a haunting message to the republican rats, the delusional clergy, and anyone mad enough to challenge their ranks, should they be suspected, even if Healy still lived. But in Rias's mind, a greater plan was unfolding.

***

"And that's how to patch a hole in your ship and keep yourselves from the bottom of the sea! Understood? Good," said Sweeney. The children exhaled in exhaustion. Swollen brains struggled to contain all the information they had received.

"Now, the bit we've all been waiting for: Merithia," Sweeney sang, as he chalked the words, *'Lesson 12.'* Neal stated he did not care anymore, so Sweeney suggested that Merithia was not so different from Cadbey. A few cadets scoffed, but their teacher was right.

Tsar Alva Olander of Artrik had ruled Merithia for fourteen years. Alva was young, charming, beautiful, cunning, and she had a loyal following. Her throne was situated in Varlden Halsstad, where the Gulf of Artarer meets the heart of Scavana. Roughly translated, this great place was called, 'the city in the throat of the world.' Earls from all over Merithia would elect a Tsar with the blessing of their people. Cadbey saw this as a sign of weakness, for a monarch reliant on votes is a monarch restrained by indebtedness. Still, Merithia's economy had boomed during the industrial revolution. Furthermore, Alva had conquered the entire southern continent of Scavana. This jagged stretch of land was three times the size of Cadbey's eight provinces. The Royal Skuas were the only reason Merithia had failed to claim territory in Arcaya. And Alva's forces no longer bolstered an invasion fleet. Now, the Oborians had the power of hycinthium-lapis and Alva had focused her intentions elsewhere, despite regular altercations at sea between merchant ships, the navy, and the Skuas.

"Merithian soldiers still rely on musket or sword. But do not underestimate their skill and strategy in battle. Merithia's presence in our waters has diminished. We're mostly taking the fight to them, to ensure they're kept at bay. But there'll come a time when a Merithian will draw his sword, and you must kill or be killed."

"Easy!" Neal blurted from the comfort of his desk, so Carla kicked the back of his chair.

"I hope your confidence prevails when you see the lynx flying high above the waves, Mr Finley," Sweeney grumbled. The Merithian flag featured the silhouette of a lynx on a white background. Its spiked ears, serpentine eyes, and pointed beard were unforgettable. It was finally time to learn about the land of fire and ash.

Sundrith, or Sundrithia, was an unforgiving land. Its arid sands had produced a tireless people, but its dark deserts had hindered their ability to flourish. Many tribes had united under a single banner held by High Sheik Kabil, named Sundrithia. Trade with Merithia had lifted Sundrithia from the dark ages, but it lacked the resources to be self-sufficient. So, Kabil was intent on developing a navy. The desert kingdom had challenged the Skuas at sea. The High Sheik wanted to learn from his seafaring enemy. He also desired a skimmer boat, so they could develop their own, but Sundrithia would struggle without hycinthium-lapis. Provoked, the Skuas had discovered docklands of warships moored in Tahlbarka, Sundrithia's capital. The armada's destination was never verified, but the night devils could not let it be. The shores of Tahlbarka were set ablaze one night, five years ago, and a hundred ships were destroyed. Sundrithia had not posed a threat since.

"Make no mistake," said Sweeney, wagging his chalk stick. "Sundrithia is imperialistic. Kabil wants nothing more than to establish a colony somewhere in the north. I mean, wouldn't you if all you could taste was sand every time you sipped your milk or whatever it is you cadets drink these days, vodka?"

"So are the raids legal or not?" Todd asked. Eyes darted, as a Witherow hooked their attention.

"Merithia has given birth to a new enemy, and our people are too blind to see it. I doubt Tsar Alva knows what she's created. Maybe we should have established a link first, instead of hunting down Merithian gold. Either way, Sundrithia is a hostility. The only thing stopping a declaration of war is their inability to agree on it... And the fact we turned their fledgling navy to ash." Some cadets gulped at the thought of a new enemy.

Panting, Sweeney wiped sweat from his brow. His cadets groaned at the prospect of another lesson. But Sweeney's final words were genuine, heartfelt, and severe.

"There's one final task I must give. From now on, you only have each other. The ocean is a vast and dangerous being. Nothing more than a few planks of wood will separate you from the abyss. And the abyss will take you regardless of whether you're an Oborian, a Merithian, or a Sundrithian." Sweeney stared at Neal, who had revealed his prejudices. "So, in the words of Major Winsford, 'look after one another, brothers and sisters alike, and you shall return, for death awaits the selfish and wicked.'" Neal refrained from making any snide comments, as the children accepted each other. "Now, the lockdown has been lifted. Tomorrow will see the funeral of Thomas Witherow, the only Skua to lose his life during the last tour. You're to report to the main hall at zero six hundred hours."

Before Todd could react, Arthur Shilling entered the room. His velvet jacket was dishevelled, his shoes were scuffed, his hair had crawled from a drowned top hat. Arthur said he had come for the boy. Neal jeered, as if Todd was in trouble, but

Sweeney gave him permission to leave. Todd demanded good news as they marched through the hall.

"We're off to see your father. There's something he needs to tell you," Arthur explained. Todd's guardian escorted him to a fine carriage. It carried them to the palace where the dungeons were located. Its confines juddered, as its wheels traversed cobbles and filth. Every bump jolted Todd's nerves. The cadet questioned his father's wellbeing, so Arthur insisted he be patient. Soon, their ride was through the main gates, and heading straight for the king's residence. The horses towing their carriage snorted at passing engines, as they entered Isabella's Square, and crossed its pale slabs. Seabirds dispersed against a grey canopy. They passed a glorious fountain, which bolstered a statue of Queen Isabella. She was guarded by her left hand, Admiral Winston Cleverly and her right hand, General Vincent Arclid. This is where Cadbey's residents would gather to hear the words of their majesty; it is where they would come to mourn the fallen, and it is where they would huddle to hear Alan's sentence. Arthur led his godson up the same marble steps they had ascended just a few days ago. But they took a different route through the palace. Shadows beckoned them into the cold depths of Cadbey's innards.

"Dad!" Todd shouted, as they reached his father's cell. He pressed his face against the rusted bars.

"Steady on, lad. You're a Skua now," said Alan. He sighed when he spotted Todd's uniform. Yet, a part of him felt proud. He asked his son if he was being looked after. Todd eagerly complimented Robert's kindness, Spike's assertiveness, and he repeated some of Sweeney's teachings. Alan bottled his temper when Todd mentioned The Swoop Inn. But he did not mention the drone bombing. The steed's bulging eyes, and the blistering blood, still tormented him.

"I know all about sabre squadron," Alan admitted. It was a squad their family had served for generations. Arthur reminded them that their time was short, so Alan insisted that Todd listen closely.

"Do you know anything about your mother, lad? Did Tom ever say ote?" Todd shook his head. Alan took a deep breath. "Your mother was a Merithian." Todd looked at his father and Arthur in disbelief. Merithia was their nemesis. He had been raised to believe nothing else. Yet, Merithian blood pumped through his veins. Alan continued, before Todd could unleash a torrent of questions. "She was accused of being a spy, and put to death, when you were just a baby."

"I... I thought she died of pox," said Todd.

"Aye, that was my first wife, Martha. God rest her soul," Alan explained. "Ya see, you and Tom don't share the same mother. You're half-brothers, lad. That's why he was nearly twice your age." Todd had never considered their age difference. Tom was his hero.

He gripped the bars and asked, "What was my mother's name... and how did you meet?"

"Your mother's name was Viveca. The locals called her Vivien, which she bloody well hated. We, the Skuas, boarded a Merithian galleon one night, in the sea of forts[20], and we took prisoners. Viveca was one of them. She was a nurse, so I had her tend ta the wounded, our sailors and theirs, not to mention myself. She treated this." Alan extended a tattooed forearm, covered in tampered flesh. "Well... one thing led to another. She defected, along with a few of her crew, swore an oath to the king, and then she swore her vows to me, in secret of course."

"Why?" Todd asked.

"A vice admiral and an ex Merithian - keep up Witherow junior," Alan demanded. Few knew the truth. Those who did could not let it be. Viveca was accused of espionage and charged with treason, not long after Todd was born. She was

---

[20] A perilous minefield of rock and forts. Merithian ships navigate its field to avoid enemy vessels.

executed in private, to protect the Skuas' dignity, and to prevent unrest. Alan took a moment to think. Then he mumbled, "That's why I've challenged the Skuas, ever since... There was nothin' I could do ta protect her. I should have known better. Her blood is on my hands-"

"Alan," Arthur muttered.

Todd understood his father's sadness, but he had to ask, "Was she a spy?"

"No, never," Alan answered, but his eyes were heavy with doubt. Arthur politely kept his silence. Todd felt confused and wished his father had said 'yes'.

"How could you marry a Merithian?" the cadet asked.

"Merithians are no different from you and me," said Alan. Mr Sweeney had taught the same out of respect for their enemy. "They're not sea demons, they don't hide under your bed at night, and there're more Scavanians living in this city then you might think. Every sailor longs for home, Todd; the touch of their loved ones." Alan had grown tired of war. Smirking, he leant forward and asked, "D'ya feel any different, now ya know you're half Merithian?" Todd took a moment to check his being. "Have any horns sprouted from your head, lad?"

"Why're you telling me this?" said Todd.

"It's important you know who you are, and how you came to be. You're a Witherow, destined to be a Sabre. The name will serve you well. But don't trust anyone. I can't say what will happen at sea, if it comes out that your mum was Merithian," Alan explained. The issue had mostly been forgotten since Viveca's trial nine years ago. But the danger was real.

"Time's up!" a guard yelled.

"You'll be at Tom's funeral tomorrow!?" Todd asked.

"The distance between us will be very, very great. But when you look up at Zora's star, the brightest point in the night sky, I'll be looking at it to, and guiding you all the way," said Alan.

"When will I see you again?" he asked.

"I'm proud of you, Todd. Never forget that." Arthur led his godson away. Todd watched as the shadows consumed his father's cell.

"Never tell anyone what you've learnt today," Arthur advised.

Their journey back to R.B.S headquarters was silent. It was evening by the time they arrived.

"How would you feel about coming to live with me?" Arthur asked, as he walked Todd to his dorm. He had challenged Winsford's law, and was fighting to gain legality over the boy, but Todd was too upset to answer. The minister tried to encourage him by boasting about garden mazes, secret rooms, and racehorses. Still, Todd remained quiet, so Arthur suggested he get some rest ahead of Tom's funeral. Abbey greeted Todd with warmth, but he paid her no attention. He climbed into bed where he could restrain his tears.

"Neal, if you say one word, I'll cut your balls off!" Carla threatened, as she made her way over to Todd. The prankster insisted he was preoccupied. She knelt beside Todd, so she could caress his hair, but he was unfazed by her touch. Carla asked if he wanted to talk, but she received no reply.

"We'll be with you every step of the way," she promised. "You're not alone." Todd feared the truth. Would she be so keen to comfort him if she knew he was half Merithian? Abbey waited hesitantly, before giving him a cuddle. Then, she jumped back into bed, so Todd could grieve in peace.

Chapter 6
The Guidance
of the Dead

"Miserable Bastards!" Sartorius blasted, before swiping a decanter across the room. Crawford winced, as the globe smashed into a thousand pieces, but neither Rias nor Grenyard flinched. Flames danced behind them, and contorted shadows flickered across the room. "I said threaten Ackerley, not kill him!" The admiral launched his drink at the fireplace. Its alcohol burst into flames. Crawford panicked when he realised the rug had caught fire, but Sartorius, blinded by rage, continued ranting from his chair.

"And could it be High Priest Healy is so divine, that he's learnt the art of resurrection? No, Howard Healy is still walking around because you necked the wrong bastard!"

"Ackerley was republican scum. He would've turned a whole generation against us. Death was the only penalty!" Grenyard insisted. He had encouraged Rias to kill Ackerley because the people lacked fear and the republicans were growing in strength.

"And how do you explain Healy?" Sartorius asked.

"What of him?" Grenyard replied. "His time will come." The people would still fear Merithia's presence following Halbert Smythe's death, restoring the need for Skua dominance.

Crawford found the courage to say, "If it's any consolation, admiral, the arrest of Sir Witherow went according to plan."

"Shut up, Crawford. If I had another glass, I'd throw it at you," Sartorius replied as he retreated into his chair. "As trusted marines you've failed to assist our power struggle. If anything, you've made it worse." Oborus, nor the republicans, would take Ackerley's death lightly. The Skuas would be suspected. Furthermore, Rias had failed to subdue the church by killing Father Halbert Smythe. Healy would seize further influence and his followers would demand a witch hunt.

Shaken, Sartorius passed Grenyard a scroll containing new orders. "Change of plan... The king has rejected a resettlement programme, aimed at relocating civilians to mine red rock. The lords need men to work the mines, and we need red rock to power our ships. We'll appease the bastards by bringing them men. We'll prove they need us," Sartorius explained. Evil flickered in his eye, as Crawford took and scanned the document.

"Sir, this letter demands a thousand P.O.Ws. Even if this many soldiers were captured... we don't have the capacity to transport this many troops."

"Who said they have to be troops?" Sartorius grunted.

"But admiral... this is slavery," Crawford declared.

"Red rock will cement our dominion over the seas. Then, we can use it to crush the enemy. We'll even be able to mount an invasion of Merithia," Sartorius snarled. His hand shook, as his aging, troubled mind wandered.

"What about the position of vice admiral?" Grenyard asked.

"Not a chance. Oswald is still out there. I can feel it. I suggest you find him. Fulfil the guidance of the dead[21], then return to sea... Get out of my sight," Sartorius ordered. Rias departed swiftly, but Grenyard remained, and growled, as the flames began to spread. "What's become of you commander? I sense a great change in you. Should I consider removing you altogether?" Sartorius queried, so Grenyard followed Rias's

---

[21] A public funeral held in Isabella's Square for fallen soldiers and sailors.

leave. Despite his flaws, Sartorius had denied Grenyard further power. Crawford stomped the rug and killed the infantile flames before leaving. Then he hid amongst a dark corridor, to conceal his dread, whilst contemplating their new mission: the establishment of slavery.

***

The midmorning sun shone upon Isabella's Square and a thousand Oborians, whose breath merged with the mist. Still, the sunlight stung Robert's eyes.

"Why do we always end up facing the sun?" he asked to relieve the tension. Spike shushed him quiet. All eyes were upon them. They would be the only squadron carrying the dead.

The Royal Skuas were stood at attention beside the palace. They were a grid of shadows on a white plaza. Torn bicorn hats, black bandanas, and polished knee-high boots gave them a fearsome appearance. Standing collars framed their blackened cravats, which had been tucked into strapped, leather vest jackets. Gloves, and decorative gauntlets, covered their forearms. Ceremonial daggers and sabres clung to their belts, alongside holstered revolvers, which had pulled their trench coats aside. Directly opposite were soldiers from the Oborian Guard. Their blue tunics, reflective boots and shakos were decorated in gold. In between was the coffin of Thomas Witherow. King Oborus, his cloaked advisors, High Priest Howard Healy, Admiral Sartorius, and General Bestla were seated on a palace balcony, high above the marble steps. Shivering, they overlooked a square of people united in grief. Yet, some had come to mock the Skuas and the monarchy. Seabirds squawked overhead, whilst using Isabella's statue as a base.

"As good a turn out as ever, your majesty," said Sartorius.

To his displeasure, Bestla replied, "I've stepped up security, so the people know they're safe."

"Safe? So you've discovered the source of the drone bombs?" the king asked. Bestla had not uncovered any culprits, despite several raids. "Then my people simply *suppose* they're safe. I want the perpetrators brought to justice." Sartorius smiled at Bestla's failure to impress the king, but his delight was short lived. "Admiral, I can't help but feel you've missed a trick." Confused, Sartorius questioned his majesty. "A hundred deaths are a statistic, where we seldom bury the dead. One death at sea, however, is a rare tragedy. It allows the people to shoulder the pain of one family. On this occasion, the father of that family is a national hero, a knight of the realm. Yet you've decided to lock him away. And now his only son, a ten-year-old boy, stands alone in the eyes of a nation."

Sartorius replied, "But the boy's father broke the law, your majesty. He defied Winsford's-"

"That may be. But this was an opportunity to regain support and compassion for the Skuas. Now all the people see is further brutality," said Oborus.

A horn signalled the guidance of the dead. Sabre squadron stepped forth and lifted Tom's coffin from a plinth. Rob insisted that Todd walk beside him.

"Head up, Todd. Let's do your brother proud. Stick with me," said Rob, with a tear in his eye. Then, they began their march through Isabella's Square. Todd was overwhelmed. A thousand citizens threw petals at his feet, whilst offering him their condolences. Barely anyone had recognized his existence. Now, he was the centre of attention. Again, Todd feared his Merithian identity. Would the people be so kind if they knew his mother had been a spy? Then, he spotted Eldrid amongst the crowd. The homeless agent nodded as a sign of trust, but Todd remained uncertain.

An arduous march led them to a burial ground on Cadbey's western shore. A thousand tombstones observed the twinkling ocean, where a thin fog lingered on the waves. Wildflowers bowed to a sea breeze, beneath the murky sky. Everyone stopped beside Martha Witherow's grave. Todd could not remember visiting her resting place, and his father had spoken little of her. Thomas would visit Martha's grave, after months at sea, but this was something he did alone since Alan had rediscovered love and loss in Viveca. Todd felt a strange emptiness consume him. Martha shared his surname, but she was a stranger. Then he spotted her engraving:

'*Martha Witherow*
Loved by all.
She longs for her husband, who serves at sea.
She longs for him still, whilst she serves in heaven
Where they will be united once again, forever more.
1753 – 1786'

Todd was born in 1793. The young boy gulped and thought, 'Has anyone noticed the dates? Would anyone even question them?' Undertakers lowered Tom's coffin into a grave beside his mother's. A priest began speaking.

Father Norbury was a young preacher desperate for praise and attention. His crimson robe, and black hair, rustled in the wind. Slender fingers clasped his bible. His rat like features protruded over its pages.

"Thomas Witherow, born June tenth, 1778, died before his time, serving his kingdom. Thomas was a fine sailor. He was brave, loyal, and daring." Many nodded as Norbury spoke. "So, it comes as a deep shock, and a tragedy, that he gave his life during an unlawful skirmish. Have no doubt, he will be judged by almighty god, as will all those who claim to serve the crown." The Sabres looked concerned. Norbury continued, "How many more daughters and sons shall we lose to mindless acts of aggression? How many more souls will reach the seabed because of nothing more than greed?" Frustration bested Rob.

"Sundrith was mounting an offensive!" Spike elbowed him quiet.

"Tom's father cannot be here today. He has been incarcerated by the same band he so ardently served. Surely, now is the time to lay down our arms and, instead, enlighten the world with the word of God," said the preacher.

"I'll enlighten him with my blade," Jared whispered, but he could not raise Ness's spirits. She would never become accustomed to death, despite her role as a Skua. A cold wind wrapped itself around them. Vested by God, the priest continued his speech, as they tried to remember Tom.

"Just yesterday, Father Halbert Smythe, who many of you will know, was killed in his bed chamber, by someone clearly masquerading as a Merithian spy." Many people gasped in shock. "He was killed, by his own kind, for Merithia *longs* for the word of Allód. They hold no grievances against our church. But first we must cleanse the corruption within our own kingdom!" Despite elbowing Rob, Spike had heard enough.

"Oi, preacher! Some of us have got a realm to protect. Wrap it up." She diverted their attention to Todd, who tried not to sob. The priest laughed in pity. He scanned her bruised eye, shaven head, and ghoulish look.

"Well, aren't you a fine example of his majesty's… finest. Tell me, are those piercings your own, or have they been looted as well?" Spike fought to keep her nerve and ignore his poor humour. Fortunately, the priest conceded. "Perhaps you're right. We should not delay the judging of the damned." Finally, Thomas Witherow was committed to the dirt. Todd felt angry. He did not want to hear about God, nor did he want to join in songs about Allód or religious sacrifice. He wanted to hear more about his brother: Tom's deeds, passions, and character. But he was gone, never to return. Alan wept for his sons from a cell far below the ground.

Slowly, the crowds dispersed. Todd wondered if any relatives might step forth; but no one stayed, and Arthur was nowhere to be seen. He was busy, fighting for the boy's freedom. Then, Todd spotted Mr Sweeney. The teacher kept his distance, paid his respects, and wished the boy good luck by raising his hand. It pained him to say goodbye. Todd, like his brother before him, was a favourite student. Too many had failed to return to Sweeney's classroom. Bereaved, Robert placed his arm around Todd, as Abbey and Carla arrived to comfort him. But a chill intervened, as Grenyard appeared like a corpse unearthed.

"So, this is Witherow's youngest." Todd stood his ground, but Abbey was petrified. "Are those tears boy?" Todd's childhood heroes bore scars. Even his dad was covered in etchings. But Grenyard's wounds had turned him evil. Todd could sense Grenyard was behind his father's imprisonment, and perhaps Tom's death.

"We'll toughen him up, sir," said Robert. Grenyard stepped forth, so Robert could smell his rotten breath.

"See to it. There's no room for frailty," he demanded. Spike and Jared watched in concern. They had not decided if they would abandon Todd, but Grenyard's manner suggested they should leave him behind. Their commander disappeared, so Eldrid approached. The caretaker had been observing them from a safe distance. Robert was surprised to see Eldrid again, but he let him join their group.

"How are you settling in, Todd?" Eldrid asked. He removed his tea-cosy hat, as a sign of respect. A thick sheepskin blanket still shielded him from the cold.

"Where's my father... why's he still in jail?" Todd replied. Rob ushered Todd towards his friends, so he could question the homeless elder. Jared, Ness and Spike listened in.

"We're doing all we can, but treason demands a quick trial, and an even swifter execution," said Eldrid.

"Who's we?" Robert asked. He understood Eldrid was a veteran, loyal to Witherow and the Skuas, but he did not understand how a drifter could influence the council. Eldrid refused to answer.

"Will you look after the boy?" he asked. Robert glanced at his comrades and Todd. Their sunken eyes remained fixed on Tom's grave.

"I'll look after him. I promise... until the sea takes me," said Rob.

"Good," said Eldrid. "The Witherow line must continue. They have served this realm for centuries, and they must serve it now, in what may be its darkest days. I must be off; time is at the essence. Alan's sentencing is tomorrow. At least the boy will not have to witness it." Rob could only watch in confusion, as Eldrid disappeared through the overgrown cemetery.

"Tomorrow," Robert whispered to himself in disbelief.

"Who's that?" Spike asked.

"I'm not sure," said Rob. "Another veteran... hanging on to the past." The Skuas headed back to headquarters, so they could prepare for departure. Tomorrow, they would set sail across the Aeternum Ocean, with or without Todd.

Chapter 7
Egress

The vast horizon birthed a timid sun, which cast brilliant rays across a turbulent sea and a restless land. Awoken, a lone skua stretched its wings and stepped down from its nest. Egg shells cracked beneath its webbed feet, as it tested its feathers, and scanned the world. Waves crashed against the towering cliff face, and the wind rustled its breast, but the seabird called out in defiance. The time had come to fly the nest. With instinctive courage, the magnificent creature hurried forth and leapt into the unknown.

Ripples lapped the sides of Spike's skimmer, HMS Sabre, which tilted and creaked, as Rob conducted his tour. Todd did his best to scribble down notes, but a tricorn hat kept blocking his vision, and a royal issue Skua dagger pulled at his belt. Their vessel boasted Gatling-gun emplacements at the bow and stern. They could tear soldiers apart with ease. Bullet chains decorated a wooden cockpit and cabin crowded with instruments. These bruised, brass contraptions reflected ammunition crates, black powder bombs, ration tins, toolboxes, and fishing rods, which left little room to rest, but true night devils never sleep. Rob asked Todd if he knew how to fish. Alan had taken Todd fishing most summers. They had ventured as far North as Silvashire, where glacial streams meet crystal lakes. Strange folk roamed its lands, wolves and bears stalked its woodland depths, but Todd had always felt safe in his father's presence. The boy realised; his dad was no longer around to protect him. He had been forced to trust the same marines who had failed his half-brother...

Rob was impressed the young boy could fish, but Todd had never killed, gutted, or cooked a catch. He would show him how to poach the finest kippers in all Arcaya! But first, Todd asked if he could see the heart of their ship. Rob lifted a sturdy hatch, behind the cabin's entrance, to reveal a battery. The metallic contraption was cylindrical and packed with refined red rock. It was a crude object, lined with cooling fins, but it contained power decades ahead of its time. Spike appeared on the harbour and summoned Rob.

"What are you doing?" she asked sternly.

"I'm familiarising the boy with the ship," said Rob.

"Well don't," Spike demanded. Oblivious, Rob could not understand her aggression. Spike disappeared to find her father, leaving him confused.

"What do they say... about my father?" Todd asked. Rob smiled at the opportunity to tell a story.

"Words don't do him justice. You must have heard the battle of storms?" Todd had read about the conflict. It had taken place in 1783, two years after Alan had been promoted to vice admiral. It was strange to his see his father's name in writing. The Skuas had clashed with a Merithian fleet in the infamous Sea of Torment. Witherow's men had braved maelstroms and tornadoes to prevent the enemy from reaching Arcaya via Sundrith. "He took down the Leviathan that night."

"My dad took down a sea beast!?"

"No," Rob laughed. "I mean the ship, the SS Leviathan. The Skuas were outnumbered five to one. You probably wouldn't have been born if he hadn't of sunk that ship." Todd's father had never mentioned his heroism. "Well, I guess it's not one for the dinner table," Rob replied. War was a terrible sin. Maybe Alan regretted his actions, after falling in love with Todd's mother, Viveca. Maybe Todd was simply too young to hear such stories.

"I don't know if I could ever be that brave," Todd muttered, as he prevented his hat from slipping. He had envied his ancestors, father, and brother; and he had dreamt of becoming a Skua, but now he was aboard a skimmer boat, and the Aeternum Ocean lay before him.

"I thought the same about myself, yet here we are," said Rob. "People aren't born brave, Todd. It's a choice we make when others need us most. Even your brother knew that, as brave as he was." Todd nodded in agreement. "Anyway, there's plenty more stories where that came from. Come on, we've got work to do!"

***

Ness shrieked, as Jared whipped her thigh with his bandana. He told Ness to be quiet, as he stalked her through the barracks with a wicked grin. They reached a silent dorm, where Jared pinned her against the wall.

"Spike will be looking for us!" Ness panted, as Jared shunned her vest jacket and unbuttoned her blouse. "We should be helping the others to prep," she said, not wanting him to stop.

"Get on the bed," Jared ordered, as he tossed his hat across the room. He would not be denied this opportunity.

"This better not be the bed of an officer," Ness said in a playful manner, before crossing its surface on her hands and knees. They were risking their lives, but the feeling was electric.

"Why, should I discipline you like one?" said Jared. She turned and began undoing his belt when she noticed a silhouette in the doorway.

"What have we here?" Rias asked in his soulless voice.

"Piss off Rias. Can't you see we're busy?" Ness shouted. She whipped Jared's belt from his waist and slammed it on the bed.

"Busy? Yes... I've been busy... we've all been busy." The barracks were silent, as Rias stepped inside the room. Jared stood up and faced him. "The time approaches. You will each have to decide if you're with us or against us." Rias slowly slipped his fishhook from his sleeve. "I do hope it's against us," he whispered.

"What the hell is that supposed to mean?" Jared growled.

"...Carry on," Rias muttered, before backing away and leaving the room. They waited until his footsteps had faded.

"Creep," Ness declared. They feared what Grenyard might do if their relationship was exposed.

"They're unhinged. We need Oswald," said Jared.

"You think he'd defy Winsford's law and show us mercy?" Ness replied sarcastically. Jared sighed in unease, though his focus was on the unit, and Grenyard's tyranny.

***

"I'm sorry, Eleanor!" Spike's father pleaded. He chased her down a jetty strewn with empty bottles, old tools, and tattered papers. Spike's ship, HMS Sabre pulled at its mooring. "I can't control what my boss charges. And I won't reveal where he lives... I don't drink as much as I used to. And when I do, it's only because I miss you... and your mother." Tony's daughter grabbed him by the neck and raised a blade to his face.

"I can smell the vodka on your putrid tongue," she growled. Rob scrambled onto the jetty, and cautiously asked if everything was ok.

"What do you think?" Spike grunted. She thrust her father away before approaching Rob. Her black eye made him feel uneasy, it had become toxic in colour.

"There's a batch of salt beef waiting for us at The Swoop. We're not leaving without it. Fetch it," Spike ordered.

"Now!?" Rob asked, as the entire regiment was preparing to leave. But the teenager did not wish to test Spike's patience.

"Fine. Keep an eye on Witherow." He set off in a hurry. Meanwhile, Todd had wrapped himself in a bullet chain. Spike questioned what the boy was doing.

"I'm practicing," said Todd. "Rob said I might have to run ammo between the guns." Spike sighed, but she had already made her decision. She approached the boy with an important mission.

"I need you to go to the barracks and fold me as many sheets as you can find. Then, I'll send Rob to help you carry them back to the ship. Understood?" Bullets clinked around Todd's neck as he pondered. He was not sure what the sheets were for, but he did not want to question Spike's authority, and her crystal eyes seemed trustworthy. The cadet removed the ammo belt, disembarked HMS Sabre, and hurried towards headquarters. Spike gave her lingering father a deathly stare, encouraging him to leave.

Robert ventured towards The Earl's Corner Club, where a line of carriages could usually be found. Oddly, not one carriage was present. Rob patted his sides in disappointment, and looked around like a lost soul, before spotting a bystander. He asked the smoking lady where all the carriages had gone.

"It's the trial of that ex-vice admiral," she shouted from her waiting spot. "It's not one to be missed. His son was buried just the other day. It's a right drama."

"Of course," Rob uttered aloud.

The gallows awaited Sir Alan Witherow, as he made his final journey. His chains grazed the floor of a twisted tunnel. His rags were putrid. But this defiant warrior would remain steadfast until the end. The light burned his eyes, as he reached an iron gate. Isabella's Square lay beyond it. 'How has it come to this?' Alan thought. The unyielding veteran had sacrificed everything for Cadbey. The Skuas had grown too powerful, too misguided, and too ravenous. Thus, Alan would pay the ultimate price for challenging their position. The thought of joining Thomas, Viveca and Martha comforted him, but his heart bled for Todd. Bestla's guards escorted him onto a stage, where the noose was waiting.

Panting, Rob fought his way through The Swoop Inn and created a space at the bar. After several minutes, the barman finally offered his services. His tattered shirt was stained in ale and sweat glistened atop his bald head. Rob insisted he had come to collect a batch of salt beef, but the piggish bartender denied all knowledge.

"Salt beef? Spike, Eleanor Archer, there's a batch of salted beef wa-"

"Look mate! Sayin' salt beef over and over again doesn't make it so. Besides, I don't owe Spike a bleedin' thing. The bitch beat one of my girls and she's always smashing up the place," he explained.

The clock was ticking, but Rob had to ask, "Beat one of your girls?"

"Took a piece of her as a souvenir... bit it clean off."

"Bit what off exactly?" The man leant forward.

"Why don't you go ask her yourself? Now, if you're not drinkin', piss off," he demanded, before tending to a customer. Robert growled and quit The Swoop Inn for the last time. He realised his task had been a distraction and that Spike was planning to abandon Todd. An ominous cloud threatened rain, and their regiment was leaving, but he had to attend Alan's trial, for the boy's sake.

The masses watched in uncertainty, as the gallows creaked beneath a fine drizzle. The noose was placed around Alan's neck, as a frosted breath escaped his lungs. A drum roll rattled. Silence permeated from winters air. Then, Alan spotted Rob through the crowd. The large sailor was on the outskirts of a mob. A chill ran down his spine, as they exchanged a hopeless glare. Alan was going to hang.

"Look after my boy," the veteran ordered with piercing eyes. Distraught, Rob barged through the crowd, fought through Isabella's Square, and disappeared in search of Todd. Then, a soldier confirmed the inevitable horror.

"Alan Witherow, born 1749, has been charged and found guilty of treason, for defying Winsford's law, and the word of his majesty, King Oborus the third, and for assaulting the king's personal guard. He will therefore hang from the neck until dead!" Alan did not wince, as a guard stepped forth to release the hatch below his feet.

"Stop this at once!" Arthur cried. The minister hurried through the crowd and clambered onto the platform. His hand waved a piece of paper, as if it were a sword. The crowd gasped and soldiers withdrew in confusion.

Exhausted, Arthur handed his note to a captain, who read it aloud. "I have a royal pardon from one of the king's advisors, signed by the king and Admiral Sartorius. This man is no longer destined to hang!" Arthur removed the noose from Alan's neck. Relieved guards let him free his friend.

The veteran croaked, "You took your sweet time!" For once, Alan had a lump in his throat. The audience rabbled amongst themselves, as the captain continued reading.

"There's more. Alan Witherow shall no longer pay the penalty of death. He shall instead be exiled to the mines of Vanth and Nadym in Terra province, where he will remain for the rest of his days." A mixed reaction erupted from the masses. Arthur had forced Sartorius's hand, thanks to his cabinet and the king's advisory. But Dead Man's Chasm was a merciless compromise.

"God damn it, Arthur!" Alan exclaimed.

"Don't start!" his saviour replied. "I have further word regarding your son. He's to live with me as his guardian. I must find him at once!"

**

Panting, Todd arrived in an empty barrack. The old building sent shivers down his spine, so he did his best not to dally. The Skuas had left their temple cold and bare. Distant tides called to them like unearthly sirens. Paranoid, the cadet began folding sheets. BUMP! He screamed as a ghoul burst from the cupboard! Petrified, he launched his sheets and buckled.

"Todd!" the ghoul shrieked. Sceptical, heart racing, Todd opened his eyes to see Abbey. She had been hiding in the dusty closet. Todd asked her what she was doing.

"I'm scared, I don't want to go to sea," she rambled. "But I don't want to go home either. My mum worked me until my hands were cracked, and my feet were blistered, ever since Pa never came back from sea." A tear rolled down her cheek. Todd returned to his feet and brushed himself down.

"We'll be ok if we all stick together," said Todd. "We need to be brave."

Abbey sniffled, "But I'm not brave. I can't even swim." Todd remembered what Rob had told him.

"No one's born brave... it's something we choose to be, when our friends need us most," said the boy.

Abbey blushed and replied, "I don't believe that... but thank you." Todd nodded and gave the girl a gentle hug. She closed her eyes in relief. Then, he asked her to help him fold sheets. They started stripping beds, which soon became a game. Alerted by giggling, Jared and Ness entered the room. Abbey halted, as if they were in deep trouble, but Todd continued his manic task.

"Todd, what the hell are you doing? Why aren't you with the ship?" Ness asked. She subtly buttoned her blouse and swiped her bloodred hair to one side. Todd paused to explain his mission, which made no sense to her. But Jared understood what was happening.

"Leave him be," Jared whispered. Ness pierced him with her emerald eyes. Her beauty made him question his morals, but he persevered. "We can't take him with us. With men like Grenyard at the helm, he won't last five minutes." Conflicted, Ness returned her focus to the helpless boy.

Rob hurtled through town like a bull. The boiler rumbled, exhaust pipes spewed steam, the red rock was burning, and

Spike's ship was ready to leave. He stormed down the jetty and clambered aboard. Spike emerged from her cabin.

"You can't leave him!" Rob huffed. "They've hung his father... they've hung Alan Witherow!" A part of Spike disintegrated. Rob had to be wrong, so she remained committed to her plan.

"He still stands a better chance on land," she argued.

"He has no one, Ellen. Not a soul!" Spike thrust Rob against the cabin.

"That's not my name." Rob's eyes apologised.

"If we leave him now, we leave him all alone in the world," he said with a lump in his throat. "Do you really think he'd do better in an orphanage? Or at the hands of some priest? A Witherow who's failed to fulfil his duty..." Arthur had claimed the boy, but the Skuas were unaware. Regardless, Todd may still be punished for defying Winsford's law. Suddenly, Jared, Ness, Abbey, and Todd appeared on the jetty. Rob breathed a sigh of relief.

"We found these two playing games in the barracks. *Didn't we Jared*?" said Ness. Spike and Jared shared a look of disappointment. Then, Todd innocently presented Spike with a pile of sheets.

"My ship is a crèche... Brilliant," Spike grumbled. They all boarded and found a place to sit. Jared patted Rob on the back and asked why he was out of breath.

Rob uttered the words, "Alan Witherow," before shaking his head. His comrade expressed the same disbelief Spike had shown. A piece of him withered. "We can't tell the boy. Not yet," said Rob. Jared agreed, though Todd suspected his father's fate.

"Sailors, we're leaving!" Spike shouted, as she revved the engine and turned their ship around. An almighty horn bellowed in the distance. It thundered off the cape and caused the waves to tremble. The Skuas had set sail, to wage a perpetual war across the Aeternum Ocean. The mothership ploughed towards The King's Mouth like a ravenous beast unleashed. Fearsome sails and Skua emblems blocked Cadbey from view.

The war horn could be heard in the deepest dungeons. Arthur and Alan closed their eyes in despair.

"I'm too late," Arthur muttered, for he knew Todd had departed. "We'll get your boy back. First, let's get you free. Hold tight."

"Well, I'm not exactly goin' anywhere," Alan spluttered from his cell. "Other than a god forsaken tomb!" Dead Man's Chasm was an infamous ravine. Countless souls had been swallowed by its abyss. But its hollow roots contained red rock. Those damned by the crown were sent to mine its hellish channels. Few accepted a wage to operate in such conditions, and even less returned. For the first time in his life, Alan was scared, so Arthur maintained his patience.

"You need to trust me, Alan. A plan is in motion, but there are opposing forces in play. A revolution could be unfolding. I'll do everything in my power to save you, your boy, and this realm."

Chapter 8
The White
Warship of
Vaasa

The Swoop Inn was bustling as usual. Eldrid looked up, as three clandestine figures approached his table. They removed their hoods, revealing their war-torn faces. They had seen Alan's sentencing, they had witnessed Tom's funeral – the guidance of the dead, and they had answered Eldrid's call.

"Well, I'll be damned. Age has not been kind," said Eldrid.

"You're not exactly an oil painting," said Niamh Griffiths.

She had emerald eyes, just like her daughter, Ness. Her crimson hair contained white streaks, like the tail of a fox. Deep wrinkles and scars lined her once delicate face, and freckles dotted her cheeks. Niamh and Laith Kader exchanged a glare, as they all took their seats.

"You two still bickering, after all these years?" Eldrid asked.

"We've come to discuss Alan," said Niamh.

But Laith confessed in a deep tone, "Niamh reckons my boy spent the night with Vanessa. Jared is far too disciplined." Jared had adopted Laith's sternness, but he was far more adventurous than his father.

Laith had been born on Sundrith's harsh sands. He remained strict, alert, stubborn, but his violet eyes were captivating. His shaven head brandished scars, which surrounded a flaming sun on his dark scalp.

Niamh rolled her eyes and said, "You're as foolish as you are stubborn." Eldrid cackled, for his assumptions were correct. How he had missed their arguments.

"I'm sure Jared means well," said Don Simpson, Robert's father. "They're not children anymore. And Ness can handle herself."

Don was an ogre of a man. His ageing muscles had set like stone. He was taller and wider than his son, but his heavy heart was not so kind. His eyes resembled chips of blue slate. A wiry beard surrounded his tired face. Waves of silk hair met its madness.

"Aye, she can handle herself. I'm more concerned about Winsford's law," said Niamh.

"Well, it didn't stop us," Don muttered.

"That was one time," Niamh mumbled. An awkward silence followed.

"Is that it?" Eldrid asked. "Ya bunch of draugrs[22]. Years ago, you'd have been eating each other's fists by now!"

"Well, I'll maim the little bastard if he comes near my house again," Niamh declared.

"Jared has strong blood. Vanessa should be honoured to lay with my son," Laith stated. Eldrid failed to contain his laughter, as the waitress delivered a round of drinks.

"Laith, if he's anywhere near as pissin' borin' and stern as you, she'd rather lay with the fishes."

"Leave 'em be or I'll bang your heads together. It's all you've argued about the whole way here. Not another word," Don shouted. Eldrid smiled. His comrades still had some fight remaining.

Arthur arrived at their table like a ghost. He removed his velvet top hat and ruffled his hair. Dark bags hounded his eyes. He anxiously sat down beside them. Eldrid copied his demeanour, before addressing his mates.

---

[22]A spirit possessing a decaying corpse.

"Alright, let's get down to it. We've not come here for a binge and a chin wag. Arthur, if you will."

"You all saw Alan's trial… I understand you're his closest friends," said Arthur.

"The man's a stubborn bastard," said Niamh.

"He's a temperamental git," said Don.

"He stands too close, and his breath is often offensive," said Laith. Eldrid gave them a look that read, 'behave'.

"Yes well, I can't help but agree with you. Either way, you're the only ones who can help him," Arthur explained.

"Get to the point," said Don.

"Alan will be transferred from Cadbey to Red Rock Citadel in a few days' time. The final stop-off is a garrison just inside Arca province called Fort Dry Cote[23]. Beyond that is where I suggest you strike, just as the convoy enters the Abalone Mountains."

"Strike he says," Niamh humoured. "Us and what army?" Despite Niamh's comment, the veterans were not unfamiliar with such an audacious task.

"Why aren't they transferring him by train?" Don asked. A steam engine, boosted by hycinthium-lapis, ran from Cadbey to Red Rock Citadel along the Western Arca Express.

"The tracks are compromised. We'll make sure of that," Arthur replied. Niamh slid a knife from her boot and stabbed the table. Their drinks jumped in alarm, but few drunkards batted an eyelid.

"This knife has spilt the blood of a hundred Merithians. But it's never spilt the blood of an Oborian," she said. Arthur gulped at its grip, which supported a skua emblem, but its pommel formed the face of a demon. Sharp quillons curved towards its blade.

---

[23] Dry Cote, meaning a dry place, is a garrison surrounded by treacherous marshes and floodplains.

"Say we do free Alan. What then? Are we supposed to join a group of merry men? Hide in the mountains until this all blows over?" Don asked.

"Yes," said Arthur. "Until the time is right."

"What happens when the time *is* right?" Laith asked.

"Aye, what do you need Alan for?" Niamh enquired, so Eldrid intervened.

"We'll have to wait and see, won't we," said the beggar, who remained spirited. "So, what will it be? Will you stick to your oaths? Or will you drift towards death, bored and wretched?" Don sighed, Niamh removed her dagger, and Laith sat back in contemplation. A revolution was brewing, and they did not wish to be caught in political games. They had abandoned death. Laith worked for a shop fixing drones, Don volunteered at a library, and Niamh ran a stable on the outskirts of Cadbey. But they could not defy their pledge:

'*...To bear true allegiance to the monarch, their heirs and successors, to safeguard the kingdom by serving the Royal Skuas until death, to protect and provide for the kingdom, by intercepting and eliminating all those who would seek to destroy us, which is to fulfil the greatest honour.*'

Alan Witherow was a true Skua, a knight of the realm, and he had been their leader throughout battle. They owed him their lives. However, their journey across Arcaya would be perilous. Treacherous paths, blood thirsty rebels, and merciless beasts would do their worst.

"Do you want to help him or not?" Arthur snapped.

"Do we have a choice?" said Niamh.

"...At the heart of all this is a ten-year-old boy, Alan's youngest child, Todd. I understand you were amongst the crowd when he helped bear his brother's coffin," said Arthur. "We free Alan. We bring Todd home..."

"What about our own?" Niamh said aloud. Their children were serving alongside Todd, though they pitied his age and dire circumstances.

Don asked, "Do we at least get paid?"

"Of course!" Eldrid quipped. "Our good friend here holds all the coppers! Five thousand for each of you. Isn't that right, Arthur?" The minister for economics reluctantly agreed. The veterans accepted their mission.

"Good. More ale. Let's nail down these ambush plans," said Eldrid.

***

Cadbey became a speck in the distance, until it was nothing more than a reoccurring dream. The Aeternum Ocean surrounded the Sabres on all sides. Todd restrained his hat with one hand, and clasped a support rope with the other, so his eyes could admire a vast spectrum of blue. The engine thundered and the sea exploded into rain, as their skimmer jumped a torrent of waves.

"You look like you've never been on a boat before!" Rob bellowed from the stern. Saltwater spears bombarded his poncho, sodden hair gripped his face, and a belt fought to keep him safe.

"I haven't!" Todd replied. "Not one this fast... or this far from shore!" Abbey punched the air, as pigtails flicked her face. "This boat doesn't even have a sail!"

The sun flickered between three masts, which towered above the mothership. Its official title was HMS Oborus, but it had been named the mothership since it had been designed to carry six skimmer boats. Dozens of sails carried the unrelenting beast, whilst four decks contained Cadbey's wrath. Windows formed an impressive stern, which stood like a cathedral. A large quarter deck housed the might of military prowess. Todd knew the galleon was exactly ninety-nine meters long. Despite royal instruction, the warship had fallen just short of one hundred meters, but it was still the largest vessel the world had ever seen. A bowsprit extended from its front, like a warrior wielding a spear. Its tip pierced the air, cutting a path towards their enemy. Slumbering skimmers lined its gunnel. Their bodies dangled above the ocean, safe in situ, where they awaited the return of their companion, HMS Sabre.

Todd was ecstatic. For a second, all his troubles had evaporated. Tremendous sails shadowed their approach and Skua emblems conquered his pupils. Then, he scanned rows of cannons, which became clear once the sun had dipped behind the galleon. Their unfathomable eyes observed the horizon. The ship was a leviathan.

"Prepare to board!" Spike shouted. Two hooks were lowered with precision. Ness and Rob attached them to the ends of their ship. Todd and Abbey watched in amazement, as their protectors darted into position.

"Sabre ready!" the Skuas screamed in unison. The chains became tort. Todd tried to peer past cannons, into a wooden structure etched in battle, but they rose too quickly. Their boat crept above the gunnel, where a group of sailors awaited them. They saddled their ship, so Spike's squad could disembark.

A sailor named Smudge took one look at Todd and said, "What age are you supposed to be?"

Smudge was thin and wrinkled. A bushy goatee hid his true age. He had tied a black bandana around his head. Tattered clothes draped his spindly frame. Sunken eyes awaited the boy's response.

"I'm thirteen!"

"It was twelve yesterday," said Rob. Abbey giggled when she realised Todd had been lying about his age. "Go easy on him. He's Witherow's youngest." Smudge asked Rob if he had heard the latest rumours.

"Sartorius denied Grenyard the role of vice admiral. He wants Oswald found," Smudge explained.

"Thank God… but Oswald disappeared without a trace the night Tom fell in Thindraka. He could have gone overboard for all we know," said Rob. Todd felt linked through his brother's sacrifice.

"Someone must know somethin' about his whereabouts. That's what the admiral's countin' on," Smudge concluded.

"At least Sartorius still has some marbles left," said Rob.

"Aye, but now Grenyard wants blood. And the mothership is his." The cogs of war were turning. Fortunately, Todd and Abbey's infectious wonder pulled Rob from his worries.

"Come on then. Let's give you two a tour," he said.

Wide eyes observed the Skuas: scaling masts, sharpening blades, and practising martial arts. A bagpipe assisted the sailors in their preparations for war.

"This is the deck. When trouble starts, you're not to be on here, understood?" Vents spewed steam past capstans, barrels, and cannons. Abbey flinched, as a hen flapped amongst its confines. Then, Rob greeted an inquisitive pig. The beast snorted and chomped his boot.

"This is Curtis. Chef would give anything to get his hands on his bacon… As would I," said Rob. Abbey questioned who the pig belonged to. "No one really. Or maybe it did belong to someone. Someone fond of pigs I imagine. You'll find all manner of beasts on this ship: chickens, goats, sheep… Spike. But Curtis here is an avid sailor." The children patted the weighty pioneer.

They continued into a busy quarter deck. A chequered floor lay ahead, which set a boundary between officers and sailors. Red rock lamps flickered within their brass holsters, where candles remained on standby. Fine carvings covered pillars that would stand until the end of time. Small windows allowed light to wash the timber.

"Up ahead is the great cabin, now Grenyard's chamber. Completely off bounds. You'll not get caught in there if you know what's good for you," said Rob. Captains, wielding packages and scrolls, delegated tasks in passing. Their coats swirled and trailed.

"Abbey!" her captain, Edward Lanoch shouted in surprise. "I thought ye'd bailed on us!" The girl was rendered speechless.

"That was my fault, sir," said Todd. "I insisted that she help me with an important task."

Lanoch smirked and replied, "Aye, is that so."

Lanoch was the captain of Rapier Squadron. His Silvashire accent was renowned and rugged. The ends of his twisted moustache glistened, and his cropped beard was silked in seawater. Anchors had been etched below his blue eyes, and tribal marks framed his face. His ginger-brown hair pricked moisture from the air, and a bear's pelt covered his trench coat.

"She's here now. That's all that matters," said Rob.

"Indeed. I see you're giving them the tour?" Rob nodded, so Lanoch turned his attention to Abbey. "Say, if any more of these boys feel like speakin' for ye, or give ye any jib, you let me know." Abbey nodded. "And here's a little secret. Our best marines are women. Don't ye forget that." Lanoch finished his sentence with a wink, which made Abbey smile.

"And the scariest," Rob muttered. Lanoch let them return to their tour.

"I'll catch you on deck, Simmo dear boy," he said.

"He didn't ask me my name," said Todd, which sustained Abbey's smile. Rob led the cadets down a creaking staircase. Cannons awaited inspection, yet their muzzles sniffed a sea breeze in want of battle. Sailors bellowed a tune, whilst upgrading a gun.

"Shoot, slash, send them away
The dogs from Scavana won't take us this day
Rush, run, row and we'll cry
For the lands of Oborus I'll fight and I'll die

*Sail, sore, straight toward prey
Into the shadows that lurk in their bay
Intercept, eliminate, provide for our king
Who rules all Arcaya and the Skuas that sing... "*

Todd listened in awe and respect. He longed to join them in song.

"This is the upper gun deck, not to be confused with the middle gun deck... or the lower gun deck... they all look the same," Rob explained. Abbey patted the cannons, as if they were mechanical beasts. "Again, you're not to be here when trouble starts. Unless you want a ringing in your ears like Mad Morris," said Rob.

"So where *can* we be?" Todd asked as his wonder began to fade.

"You'll see. Remember, this is a warship. You're not in Cadbey anymore," said Rob.

They passed an enormous mainmast, which delved through the ship like an ancient root. Rabble and steam escaped the large grate around it. The children stared into its depths. A cauldron was boiling below a brick cook house, where sailors had gathered to share a sea broth. They descended another narrow staircase; the beams whining beneath their feet. Cobwebs caused Abbey to duck in revulsion, but they eventually reached their sleeping quarters in the belly of the ship.

Their musty chamber offered an assortment of torn hammocks and fabric screens. A vent posed as a skylight, but their den was dark, overcrowded and claustrophobic. Names and sketches had been engraved into the walls. They did little to inspire memories of home. Warped windows restricted light from leaving an adjacent passage.

"I preferred the other barracks," Todd admitted.

"Be thankful you've a room!" said Rob. "All we get is a matt and whatever space we can find." Abbey hoisted herself into a hammock. She suggested Todd could have the one above her. He failed to spot Carla's possessions.

"Now, the older cadets will have to maintain the cannons, fetch materials for the armourer and tailor, that sort of thing. As for you two, you'll be expected to mop."

Abbey whined, "That's all I was ever made to do at home!" Abbey's mum would work her to the bone, contempt that she alone had been burdened with her existence.

"Well, you should be good at it then," said Rob.

"You said I could carry ammo back and forth," Todd argued. "I've even been practicing!" Rob laughed in bemusement.

"Look, I know the first few weeks will feel strange. But this is for your own good. Soon enough, you'll be up there, on deck with the rest of them, and then you'll be wishing you were back down here, where it's safe..."

"I hate mopping," said Todd. He scuffed the floor with his shoe.

"You'll hate Grenyard's cane a lot more," Rob warned.

*****

The sun had fallen, and its orange empire was fading. Extended shadows crept across deck. Stars were surfacing; they raged amongst the night sky, and Zora's star soon appeared in the northern hemisphere. Todd observed its brilliance, in remembrance of his father. 'When you look up at Zora's star, the brightest point in the night sky, I'll be looking at it to, and guiding you all the way.' Yet, Todd's heart sank. He felt irrelevant and confused, and he could not be sure where his destiny would take him. So, he listened to a group of Skua captains who taunted each other, whilst neglecting their duties on deck. They were seated on barrels; warmed by lanterns and booze.

"Aye, Abbey's a wee skinny las, but she's got spirit, just like any Rapier. She could be the next Spike in the making!

Your Gregors on the other hand. He's a lanky streak a piss. You'd be better off usin' him ta clean the cannons with," Lanoch joked. The Skuas had commenced their annual grilling of the newest cadets. Embarrassed, Gregory dropped his head. His captain, Eva Swinton came to his aid.

"I remember when you were a boy, Lanoch - not that much has changed. You used to quake at the sight of a mere fishing vessel," said Eva, before gulping a bottle of vodka.

Her trench coat draped the barrel beneath her, and a bicorn hat shadowed her face. A spider's web had been tattooed into her hairline, and a flying skua had been tattooed on her back, so the tips of its wings reached up her neck. Lustrous black hair fled down her coat. Gold piercings lined her ears, which twinkled in the lamp light. Scarred brows complimented her onyx eyes, and her broad nose had been broken.

"Aye, that was until ye turned me into a man," Lanoch boasted, before gesturing a large pair of breasts. The other sailors laughed and jeered. Spike attracted their attention, by spitting tobacco at the floor. She was perched on a net belonging to the main mast. Lanoch's comment had rustled her jealous feathers. George Aldridge, leader of Foil Squadron, had instigated the gathering. He questioned Spike, after noticing her displeasure.

George was a noble, charismatic sailor, who aspired to be a lieutenant. He wielded confident looks, stern features, and thick bristles. His brown eyes burned with tenacity.

"What about you, Archer? I hear you've adopted the last remaining Witherow. First impressions?" George asked. Todd's ears perked up, but Carla stole his vision, by standing beside George as his latest student. A sea breeze attacked her ribs, motion sickness caused her stomach to turn, but she could not leave the initiation.

"My impression is that Lanoch should look after his cadet, and I'll look after mine," said Spike. She was referring to Abbey's abandonment, after Todd had found her hiding in a cupboard.

"Rob's been doing the baby sitting. Besides, your ship?" Lanoch quipped. "I heard Jared has been made captain." Spike knew he was lying.

"We'll see about that. Either way, it's *my* ship," she replied. Suddenly, the air changed. Rias sauntered towards them. Neal followed closely behind. Rias hated his new student, but he would not defy Skua tradition. His double-breasted coat swayed in motion, and his arctic eyes glinted in the moonlight.

"Look what the cat dragged in. Have ye come to cheer Spike up?" Lanoch asked, drink splashing in his tankard.

"I could do more than cheer her up… if it wasn't for her dirty secret," said Rias. His cold, unwavering eyes were fixed on Spike. Eva coughed in unease, but Spike was unfazed by his prejudice. She had found the courage to approach Eva when they were young, but Eva had rejected her. It was the only time Spike had endeavoured to find a partner.

"Why don't you tell us a few secrets, Rias. What's Grenyard had you doing, besides rolling over and playing fetch?" Eva asked.

"The biggest threat to our kingdom is not out there," said Rias. He raised his finger to the horizon. "It's within our own walls. When Arcaya reaches its full potential; you'll understand." Frost left their lungs, as the cold embraced them.

"So, you know who deployed the drone bombs then. Who was it?" Spike asked. She jumped down and approached him. "Republicans, the Ebony Knights[24], members of the right hand[25]?"

"Little sparrow," Rias replied. "I'd stay hidden if I were you. Not everyone in your squad is pure blood." Todd gasped amongst the shadows. Rias was referring to Jared, who had come from Sundrith, but Todd's Merithian descent may have

---

[24] A band of rebel's led by Peter Aggus and his son, Oscar, who lay claim to rule over Ebonshire.
[25] General Ernest Bestla's Oborian Guard.

been revealed. A smile spread across Neal's face, who relished the idea of an 'Arcayan' unit.

"Well, aren't ye a barrel of laughs. Ye nay fail ta brighten the mood do ye. Did ye mother not love ye as a wee baby? With a name like Zacharias, I should think not," Lanoch jabbed. The Silvashireman swigged his ale and held his stare. Unbroken, Rias departed with Neal in tow.

George whispered, "Have you never heard?"

"Heard what? Entertain me," Lanoch slurred.

"Rias was an orphan," said George. "He was found washed ashore by a priest. No family, no belongings, no past, as if the ocean simply spat him out."

"Aye, I've heard that bollocks before. So what, most of us are orphans," said Lanoch. "N' I've washed up on more beaches then I care to remember."

"Yeah, except the priests exiled him. Couldn't wait to be rid of him. As if he were a curse," said George.

"That's no excuse for being an arsehole," Eva muttered. "You ok, Spike?" But Spike had left. Lanoch disappeared to refill his cup, so Carla joined Todd.

"Carla!" he exclaimed in joy.

"One moment," she requested, before vomiting overboard. Todd winced as a jet of puke quit her mouth. She wiped her lips and checked to see if anyone had noticed. Skimmer boats swayed beside them, the sun had perished, and the horizon was barely visible.

"Ugh... Maybe I'm not cut out to be a sailor after all," said Carla, as a chill afflicted her bones. Todd could not find the words to comfort her. She knew he was grieving. "Come here little sabre. Help keep me warm." She pulled Todd close, so they could huddle together in their ponchos. Todd felt paralysed. "What's the matter? Have you never hugged a girl before?" Carla swept hair from her delicate face. Todd had never hugged his own mother, never mind a girl. He quickly placed his arm around her quivering waist. She asked him what he was doing, all alone on deck. Todd was thinking about his father and their final moments. He did not mention Viveca or his Merithian identity. Carla found it abhorrent that their last conversation should take place in a dungeon.

"He told me to gaze upon Zora's star. That he'll be guiding me... I think he's dead, Carla. Why else would he say such a thing? I want to ask my squad if they know what's happened, but I'm scared what they might say."

"What difference does it make?" Her bluntness stunned him. "You're a Skua now. *We're* your family. Your life is at sea." Todd dropped his head in thought, so Carla continued. "Do you have any idea how much weight your name carries? The Witherows have protected this kingdom for centuries. You're a guaranteed knight of the realm!" Their guardians laughed in the background, as liquor continued to flow. "Your father *can't* let you forget that. That's why every time you look at that star, you remember you're a true sabre!" Zora twinkled in the north.

"But what if I can't live up to the name-"

"You will." Carla dashed any doubt. "You're still young. But one day you'll be big, and strong, and full of heart. Just you wait and see." A smile appeared on Todd's face, so Carla hugged him tight. Her frame shivered violently, so she kept talking.

"When I was an orphan, we would speak in vain about belonging to a name like Witherow; hoping someone, anyone, would take us away. The Skuas have given me an opportunity to be something; to make a name for myself-" Carla jumped up and puked down the side of the galleon.

"HEY!" A sailor bellowed from below, for his smoking pipe had been doused. Carla laughed, despite her nausea. Todd admired her spirit and strength, but her sickness had worsened.

"Come on, let's head back to the barracks," Todd insisted.

"Why, Sir Witherow. Lead the way," Carla humoured, but her gesture escaped Todd. "Hey, remember what I said.

You're not alone. Got it?" Todd nodded, so they made their way into the depths of the ship.

***

Groans escaped the galleon, as it inhaled and exhaled. A hammock waited in a corner of the hull, where webs connected crates and barrels. Spiders scaled their silk ropes in search of prey. Chomping escaped two goats, who were tied to a beam. They looked up, as Jared and Ness appeared with a red rock lamp.

"This it?" Ness asked. She despised livestock, from being made to clean her mother's stable. Jared knelt beside his hammock with pride.

"This is the finest hammock in the unit!" he boasted. Jared had lined it with superb pelts, which he had purchased whilst ashore.

"You do realise nothing's gonna happen," Ness grumbled before slipping her boots off. A loud oink escaped Curtis, who appeared and rested his head atop a barrel. "Piss off, Curtis. And keep your trotters off our rations," Ness complained. But her emerald eyes shined, meaning nothing could destroy Jared's smile. Curtis took his leave as they removed their coats and curled up in the hammock together, where they shared a bottle of wine. Snug, Ness asked Jared if he had seen his pa, Laith.

"I did... he wouldn't stop banging on about Sundrithia and how grateful we should be. His house is full of wretched drone parts from the workshop. I nearly had to sleep next to one of those things." Ness longed for a bedtime story, so she quizzed her lover about his past. She found the deserts fascinating. At first, he gladly reminisced.

"I remember, the air always felt scorched. And the night sky was always full of stars. Far more than what you see in Cadbey. I remember, we had to sleep off the ground. At night, you could hear the sand wanderers scurry across your tent."

Ness shuddered at the thought of such arachnid creatures. Jared's tone changed. "I was four or five when my father set sail for Arcaya. A rival tribe burned our village to the ground, killing my brother, and my mother. We were the lucky ones, though it never felt that way…" Ness remained quiet, so Jared continued. "The deserts would have eaten us alive. So, my father loaded us into his fishing vessel. We drifted for days…weeks maybe…thirsty and starving. Until we were picked up by the Skuas. All my father could do was offer his service. Little did we know, I'd have to serve as well. But the Skuas saved us that day. My father proudly fulfilled his oath, and I shall do the same…" Ness snored, so Jared stopped and sniggered. He wanted to tell her that he loved her. Instead, he shut the lamp and joined her in peace.

***

For a second, Todd was home. The boy expected to hear his dad fumbling pots and pans downstairs. Only the ocean rumbled beneath his bed as he awoke. He opened his eyes to a muddle of amateur engravings. The planks above his hammock resembled a memorial, with no room for his own art or name. Light rays, from the adjacent passage, breached the barracks through a row of grubby windows. Yawning, Todd pulled his curtain aside to reveal a dust field floating in the sunlight. Abbey whined so Todd shushed her quiet. Carla was still asleep and recovering from sea sickness. They shuffled into their uniforms, which had been placed at the ends of their hammocks. Then, the two explorers exited the barracks.

Blankets and mattresses had been strewn across an unforgiving floor. Grisly characters observed them, but most remained asleep or bedridden. Their noses carried them below, where the cooking station could be found. A cumbersome chef hovered over a cauldron of stew, which had been lowered into a brick fire-pit.

"Crickey, you little nippers are up early!" the man bellowed. He seemed mad and full of charisma. A stained apron dangled from his neck, and his shirt was plastered in splodges. A ladle ruffled his moustache as he sipped and spoke.

"I reckon this is just about ready. I guess you two can have first serving!" Delighted, Abbey and Todd claimed a bowl each. The chef directed them to a stack of bread, where they tore away two healthy clumps. "I know you're new so remember, military parade is at 8am!" the cook shouted. "And let me know if you spot Curtis. I'll be damned if that pig cooks before I get my hands on him!" Excited, the cadets ventured up top.

They shuddered as they finished their breakfast. A few sailors had survived another gruelling night shift. They scaled the masts like phantoms; their silhouettes cast against the sunrise. Seabirds squawked, as waves lapped the galleon. Satisfied, Abbey suggested a game of hide and seek. A contagious mischief infected them.

"Ok," said Todd. "But we're not allowed in the officers' quarters. Let's hide on deck until it's time for parade." Abbey agreed and began counting! Surprised, Todd sprinted to the other end of the ship. After much consideration, he clambered aboard HMS Sabre and hid inside a trunk, where he nestled into a blanket. For a moment, he was safe. Its fur felt soft against his face. But he jolted, as if struck by lightning, when the inevitable occurred.

A Skua yelled from his nest up high, "The lynx flies, starboard side!" A deep war horn reverberated throughout the ship. Todd pushed against the lid, but it was locked.

"Abbey!" he cried, but she was nowhere to be found. A plague of Skuas emerged and hurried to the gunnel, where they extended their telescopes. Jared counted one, two... five ships near the horizon. Neal's courage escaped him, as he stared at the ocean in horror. Its waves became agitated, and the sky became bruised. Their uniforms thrashed against the coming storm.

"Stations!" Crawford bellowed from the quarter deck. He appeared before layers of sails, which struggled with the wind.

"Grenyard's lost his mind. We've no support and a storm stirs to the east," said Lanoch, before slamming his telescope shut.

"The Skua flies, portside!" The crowd made their way across deck. A frigate[26] flying the Skua emblem appeared in the distance. Crawford burst onto the deck.

"All squadrons prepare for launch!" he ordered. Jared joined the lieutenant's stride, where he tried to deter him from battle.

"We're outnumbered. This is another suicide mission!" But Crawford's orders were final.

The impatient lieutenant turned and said, "Are you a Skua or a navy dog? Get in your ship, serve your king." Jared contained his anger, and Crawford continued his path.

"Saddle up. We need your mettle," Spike demanded. She extended her hand and helped him aboard HMS Sabre. Ness and Rob joined them, as the other Skuas manned their attack boats.

"Lift the ramps!" Crawford bellowed, as thunder crackled in the distance. Smudge and his grunts began turning a row of capstans. Ramps, both sides of the galleon, were winched into a horizontal position, as if the mothership had wings. Then, the skimmers were lowered onto the platforms, creating an unholy concerto of wood and metal. Every captain announced that they were ready for launch. Spike and Jared shouted this at the same time, causing unease. Tumorous clouds flashed and boomed, unleashing a downpour. So, their engines ignited, obliterating the storm as they roared in desperation for war.

---

[26] A warship built for speed and maneuverability.

"Drop the ramps!" Crawford screamed, water cascading off his bicorn hat. The ramps were lowered towards the back of the galleon. Rain drenched the battle ready Skuas, who had fastened themselves in. Spike clasped the wheel and prepared for the plunge. A turbulent, blue tundra awaited them.

"Suck it up!" she shouted. They waited on the edge of oblivion.

"Launch!" Crawford ordered, which triggered a release of levers. The vessels were placed in free fall. Spike's ship hurtled past rows of cannons and crashed into the sea. Her craft shattered a wave and sped off, leaving the galleon behind it. Further boats pierced the ocean. Rob spat seawater, as the deep chilled his bones.

"It never gets any easier does it," his teeth chattered.

"Shut up and ready the gun," Jared ordered. He flung his seatbelt aside and quit a waterlogged seat at the stern.

Their boats formed an arrowhead. Sabre Squadron, led by Spike Archer, and Rapier Squadron, commanded by Lanoch, created its left flank. Falchion Squadron, led by Eva, and Claymore Squadron, spearheaded by Rias, formed its right side. George Aldridge and Foil Squadron were at its tip. Lightning lit the sky, and the sea began to swell, as the enemy drew near. Their ally, a blood thirsty Skua frigate, joined with haste. Rob asked who was commanding the ship.

"Maybe it's vice admiral Oswald Leonard, come to rescue us," Ness shouted sarcastically, whilst manning the Gatling-gun on the bow.

The Skua frigate was commanded by Vincent Blezard, who roamed the eastern sea front in search of prey. He had seen the mothership and sensed an opportunity for bloodshed. His vessel was not equipped with skimmer boats, but his crew were cut-throat, daring, and organized. Blezard, like Grenyard, was known for his cruelty.

"I can tell you who sails our enemy's ship," Jared shouted, whilst preparing a casket of black-powder bombs. The magic soot glistened between his fingers. They observed the largest

Merithian galleon: a grand display of silk paint, splendid carvings, and gold leaf. Its sails supported an array of brilliant white flags featuring the lynx. Their serpentine eyes were clear and daunting. Further flags presented the crest of a moose. "That fine ship belongs to Victor Skarsgard of Vaasa. The young Earl must be here to prove himself." Jared recognised the ship from an encyclopaedia. Plus, its distinct carvings presented Vaasa in all its glory.

"Let's take his cargo and send his ship down," Spike commanded. Rob fed a bullet chain into his Gatling gun, at the stern of the ship. Then, a ravaging chill encouraged him to dry off. Sniffling, he turned to a trunk and unlocked it. He screamed in alarm, as Todd burst from its confines.

"What in God's name!?" Rob shouted at the jack-in-a-box. Todd tried to explain himself. "We're off to war, Todd! War! You shouldn't be here!" Ness and Jared appeared either side of Spike's cabin.

"We have to turn around!" said Ness. She grabbed a support rope, as a wave pelted them.

"No way!" Spike shouted over the engine. "We're not abandoning the unit!"

"She's right," said Jared. "If we turn back, the attack will fail, the unit could perish!"

"I can run ammo back and forth. Just like I practiced," Todd suggested. Rob considered putting Todd back in the trunk, but he would drown if they were cast overboard. Fretting, the teenager placed him in Spike's cabin.

"Don't move!" Rob ordered. "And close your eyes!" He sincerely feared for the boy's life. Todd realised he was in grave danger when a symphony of cannons erupted. The skimmers shifted into a scattered formation, as shells burst the ocean. The night devils were too rapid; they were soon under Merithia's scope.

"Fire at will!" Spike screamed. Rob and Ness activated their gun emplacements. Todd covered his ears, as bullet casings flooded the ship. The stench of gunpowder consumed him, until he could no longer smell the sea. Blezard's frigate entered the fray and its cannons provided suppressing fire. Spike and her comrades would have to act fast, or the allied vessel would be torn apart. Elegant carvings burst into splinters, beautiful windows shattered into ash, and crisp sails became torn, as they zoomed past Skarsgard's galleon. Return fire punched HMS Sabre, causing it to miss Rias's boat by inches, as they swarmed the fleet like hornets.

"Jared, you ready!?" Spike asked, as they circled back around. Waves tried to throw them off course, but their engine rattled in defiance. Jared finished attaching a fuse to a sticky sack of black powder. Wide eyes observed the unstable package, which had been caked in tar. The sapper signalled he was ready. Adrenalin fuelled, Rob and Ness reloaded. Rain and salt-spray lashed their uniforms. Thunder and cannon fire roared above the ocean's growl. But they could no longer feel the bite of the sea. "How're you doing, kid?" Todd nodded anxiously. Ravenous, Spike drove them back into the chaos. Gunfire and screams resonated around them, as HMS Sabre stopped alongside the second largest galleon. Cannons extended overhead. Timber absorbed bullets, as the smog tried to conceal them.

"Keep 'em off me!" Jared shouted. He clambered onto the gunnel. Their tactics did not favour stormy seas. Two cannons retreated, to be replaced by a hydra of muskets. But Rob could not angle his turret! Fearing death, he climbed onto the gunnel beside Jared, and stuck his revolver inside the opening. Gunshots caused blood to spray from the hatch. Composed, Jared planted his sticky-bomb on the galleon. Then, he revealed a match and a bottle of sulphuric acid. Ignoring battle's cry, he uncorked the bottle and dipped the tinder, causing it to ignite. The sea tried to throw him, bullets tried to shake him, but he held his nerve and lit the fuse.

"GO, GO, GO!" he bellowed. Spike hit the throttle, causing everyone to stagger. Projectiles narrowly missed their escape; the waves spat in anger. Then, an almighty explosion challenged the storm. The galleon ruptured into flames. Timber was cast high into the air. The inferno faded into a gushing cloud of smoke. Finally, the ocean rooted through its body, pulling it under. Trapped souls would never see the light of day again. Todd felt relieved, even as burning sailors plunged into the sea.

Two blasts ripped another ship in half. Skimmers fled the decimated vessel. Only three Merithian galleons remained, including Skarsgard's White Warship of Vaasa. Plumes of smoke billowed into the air, wreckage spiralled from the sky into a swell of debris, and the rain turned ash into sleet, as if the apocalypse was upon them.

No longer outnumbered, Blezard's frigate seized the opportunity to board Skarsgard's battleship. Their ships became entangled in a frenzy. Amongst the bloodshed, Spike noticed Claymore Squadron, scaling the white galleon. Rias ascended the rope of a grappling hook, as if he had a death wish. The wind bombarded him, and a vicious conflict raged overhead, but he did not falter. Todd watched in horror and awe, as the warrior clambered aboard, and began slaying Merithians. Their white uniforms and dragoon helmets were easily identifiable across the drifting field of battle. They could not parry the Skua or his formidable fighting technique. Rias unloaded his revolver; struck, slashed, and sliced with his sabre, before reloading in a heartbeat. Todd watched the hardened children of Scavana fall. A hellish display followed. Blood spilled from the white galleon painting its sides red.

The bloodbath was far from over. Black sails entered the arena; Grenyard's mothership had arrived. Its commander watched in disdain, as Blezard challenged Victor Skarsgard's elite guard. But Grenyard knew Rias had made it aboard.

"Shade the ocean red," he snarled as he hounded the deck.

Abbey burst into the barracks where Carla was resting.

"Carla! Wake up!" she pleaded, before pouncing on the teenager. A few cadets cowered beside each other. Carla questioned what was happening. "The Merithians are here and

Todd's on deck, but I can't find him anywhere!" Afraid, Carla smudged her eyes and stumbled to her feet. She was still wearing her uniform, which made her skin look ghostly.

"Come on!" she insisted, before grabbing Abbey's hand. They made their way to the upper gun deck, where sailors were loading cannons.

They braced in trepidation when a sailor shouted, "FIRE!" Abbey let out a chilling scream, as the guns exploded. Trembling, they hurried into the rain. A vile wind parted lagoons, as riflemen lined the gunnel. A Merithian galleon rode the waves in a bid to stop their advance. Its cannons were parallel with the mothership.

"Ready! Aim! Fire!" Crawford bellowed. Merithia instantly retaliated. A hail of bullets peppered their offensive. Carla gasped, as a Skua plummeted and hit the deck beside them. She tried to cover Abbey's eyes, but they spiralled to the ground. They spluttered amidst the saltwater. Then, Carla felt a presence looming over them. A cane slammed the boards. Shaking, Carla looked up to see Commander Grenyard. Rain ricocheted off his eye patch, his scarred face offered no solace, his black trench coat thrashed behind him. Grenyard seemed to be the storm's epicentre.

"Skuas do not fall from masts. His body will be cast overboard like a heathen. You'll follow him unless you start loading those cannons!" Terrified, Carla took Abbey's hand and led her towards a stationary gun. She took a cannon ball in her quaking arms.

"Carla I'm scared, I want to go home," Abbey blubbered, soaking wet. Smudge came to the rescue. The all-seeing crow removed the ball from Carla's hands.

"Wait until Grenyard retires. Then make your way below deck!" His rattish features did not reflect his kind soul.

"We need to find Todd! Abbey said he's on deck!" Carla yelled. Smudge insisted that the boy was nowhere to be seen. Gregory and Neal arrived to assist him.

"You're of no use. Piss off and take the runt with you!" Neal shouted, whose words cut like ice. He and Gregory continued loading shots. Grenyard had left, so Carla led Abbey back towards the quarter deck. Infuriated, and shaken, she failed to notice that the riflemen had taken cover.

Todd watched from afar, as cannon fire struck the mothership. Remains rocketed from splintered wood and smoke. Todd's blood ran cold, but he could not dwell on the attack. A Merithian ship was swinging into position, so it could deny Blezard's boarding party. HMS Sabre had to intervene. Their boat soared through singed scum and remnants. Within minutes, Jared and Eva had planted a bomb on their target's stern. Another rehearsed escape followed.

Now, only two ships remained. Spike circled Blezard's frigate and Skarsgard's vessel. Her stomach locked when the second Merithian warship came into view. The beast had abandoned its attack on the mothership, and it had moved parallel with the white galleon, creating a channel.

"The bastards must be attempting to board. Jared, grab a light! We go again!" Spike ordered. Gunfire pelted her cabin and broken glass showered Todd. Ness and Rob opened fire, as the other skimmers arrived in support. Jared prepped another fuse and prayed that they would be victorious. Their eardrums pleaded for mercy, as Sabre Squadron sailed between the galleons. Corpses splashed into the waters beside them, as Jared stepped onto the gunnel. He pressed his bomb against the ship. Heroically, he ignored gunshots, sparked a match, and lit the fuse. But as he turned, the cannons erupted above him. HMS Sabre was thrown against the hull, as Skarsgard's ship burst into flames. The Sabres were flung to the ground, and Rob was hurled into the sea! Spike clambered to her feet, so she could regain the wheel, but stars blinded her vision; a high-pitched ringing repelled any sound; even Todd's screams went unheard. The Merithians had decided all was lost. They would rather sink their Earl's ship, then risk it being captured. Spike reached for the throttle. But as her fingers glanced its surface, Jared's bomb exploded. A burning nebula, entangled with debris, engulfed HMS Sabre. Crawford watched in horror from the mothership, as fire concealed the scene.

"God have mercy," he uttered. He could not bear to witness Sabre Squadron's demise. Still, he stared into the inferno, hoping they would reappear.

The flames receded. HMS Sabre bobbed between the two doomed galleons. Towering flames crackled either side and the sea mimicked lava, causing the rain to hiss. Todd opened his eyes, slowly. He had been cast like a ragdoll to the back of the ship. His vision was blurred, but he could see Jared. The broken sailor tried to stand against the starboard side. Helpless, he coughed blood down his pierced body. The rain failed to sooth his wounds. Suddenly, a Merithian sailor landed on the cabin with a thud. He had leapt from Skarsgard's fated galleon. A mohawk protracted from his helmet, and his white tunic was smothered in ash. Delusional, the sailor pulled a sabre from his belt, jumped down, and thrust it through Jared's stomach!

"No!" Todd shrieked, as Jared choked and slumped to the floor. The boy reached for his dagger, but it was missing. The Merithian removed his sword and turned to face Todd. The murderer snarled like a man possessed. Soot and blood stained his teeth. Then, he made for the boy. Todd covered his eyes and awaited the sting of death.

Chapter 9
The Tide Rises

Rias swooped down and plunged his blade into the Merithian's neck. They crashed into Spike's cabin, kicking and screaming. Rias removed his dagger, in a deceitful act of mercy, before butchering his foe. Todd looked away, but he could still hear the tear of flesh. Rias rose to his feet, blood drenched, and turned to face Todd. Arctic eyes pierced the boy's soul.

"Remember this day, Witherow." Shaking, Todd felt surprised when Rias helped him to his feet. A swirling cloud of embers surrounded them. Burning sails thrashed in vain. This was no place for a ten-year-old boy, yet here he stood consumed by death. Spike spluttered as she awoke.

"Rise little sparrow," said Rias as he took the wheel. "We're not out of the woods yet." Todd stumbled towards Jared, before leaning against the cabin. Ness was already knelt beside his corpse. Her blistered hands caressed his face, as she whimpered his name. But Jared's eyes were lost and empty. She jolted, as Rob burst from the ocean, gasping for air.

"Rob!" she shouted. A brief struggle brought him aboard, and the sea followed. Rob laid eyes on Jared's body. He screamed in agony, forcing Ness to comfort him. Defeated, he slumped his head into his companion's shoulder.

"Todd!" he then croaked. Rob looked around and beckoned the boy. "Thank God you're ok," he cried, as he placed his hand on the back of Todd's head. Rias observed them from the cockpit.

"Be thankful you'll not have to answer to Winsford's law," Rias told Ness. She growled in revulsion, as he accelerated them away from danger.

Vincent Blezard's men returned to their frigate. Few prisoners were taken, and Skarsgard's bounty was lost to the depths. Galleon carcasses danced and collided, causing the ocean to gurgle. Infernos faded into mountains of smoke. Finally, the storm drowned any signs of battle.

"Give me the wheel," Spike demanded, though she lacked the strength to confront Rias.

"Settle down little sparrow. Go see to your crew. After all, they're *your* crew now. That's what you wanted, isn't it?" Rias asked. With Jared gone, Spike would be made captain, but she snarled in repugnance. She staggered over to her fractured family. Rob looked up in despair.

"Wrap and bind him," Spike ordered.

"No," Ness whimpered. But when Rob tried to comfort her, she pushed his hand away. They wiped their tears and concealed Jared's body, using sheets taken from a nearby crate. Trembling, Todd looked up at Spike. Her crystal eyes were wild. Then, she handed him his Skua dagger. The blast had ripped it from his belt. Todd received the weapon, whilst wondering if he could have saved Jared.

"That is yours to keep," she said with a nod. Todd had been accepted, but guilt still plagued his mind.

The mothership had moved to the outskirts, so HMS Sabre followed, and the other skimmers joined their voyage. Scorches, gashes, and gouges were clearly visible. They feared the worst.

Spike's crew stepped onto a haunted deck. Smog brushed its surface and lingered over the fallen, who had been lain beside each other like mannequins. A sailor tossed a bucket of water, to wash away the blood, for the rain would not be enough. Rob noticed Crawford, knelt in despair beside the deceased. He clutched Abbey in his arms.

"Abbey...ABBEY!" Lanoch shouted from his boat. The marine leapt onto the mothership and shoved a sailor aside. Sabre squadron hurried over.

"Todd," Abbey sobbed, causing the boy to kneel beside her. He gave Crawford a deathly stare.

"She's ok," Crawford assured. For a moment, his insufferable pride had perished. Abbey was petrified, sore and bruised, but she was intact. "Carla..." the lieutenant muttered. "She fell... shielding Abbey from cannon fire." Their eyes, wishing to be deceived, fell upon a bloody blanket. Carla's contorted remains had been wrapped in the casing. Todd was unable to breathe. He remembered their embrace; the words they had spoken the night before, and the courage she had given him. Carla's captain, George Aldridge appeared from battle. Devastation swelled in his eyes.

"Where's Jared?" Lanoch asked. Rob shook his head, causing bloody seawater to leak from his hair.

Lanoch crouched beside Crawford and growled, "Was it worth it, lieutenant?" He snatched Abbey from his arms, as if she were his own daughter. Before he could leave, Grenyard appeared on deck, and Blezard's frigate pulled up alongside them.

Blezard's sailors looked hellish. Blood-stained trench coats flickered in the wind. Frayed bicorn hats hid their gruesome faces. Vincent Blezard appeared disillusioned yet vigilant. The middle-aged man did not resemble a commander fresh from victory. Todd felt unnerved by his thin hair, distant eyes, and slack jaw. The tip of his sabre held seven Merithians hostage.

"Do you want them, commander?" he bellowed. Grenyard did not reply, for the answer was obvious. "Alright then, have your soddin' fun. Come on you inbred bastards, get a move on, we haven't got all day. We've got more of you to kill!" A bridge was lowered, connecting both ships, so the prisoners could cross. They had been stripped of their jackets, and their hands had been tied. Their boots had been pulled from their feet, revealing white trousers half scorched. Todd pitied the men who looked frightened, drained, and undignified. Then he gasped, as the seventh prisoner blurted his prayers, before jumping into the ocean. A splash signalled certain death. His comrades wept in sorrow and envy after crossing the ravine.

"At least one of you has some guts," said Grenyard. He ordered Rias and his squad to bind the prisoners into one mass.

"I get the next lot!" Blezard shouted. The bridge was raised and his ship disappeared into the storm. Rias began emptying a barrel of rum over their captives, prompting them to splutter and beg.

"Spike, give me Todd. I'll take the cadets down below," said Lanoch, still holding Abbey. But Grenyard overheard him.

"Captain... bring them here," he snarled. Lanoch hesitated and closed his eyes in regret. "Captain... don't make me ask you again." Lanoch growled, took Todd's hand, and walked the cadets over to their commander. Todd looked Grenyard in his demonic eye. "Your naivety has cost lives. Now these men must pay... severely," Grenyard lied. Sabre Squadron were sickened, but Spike grabbed Rob's wrist to stop him from intervening. Rias threw the empty barrel aside. Then, one of his men passed Grenyard a flaming torch.

"Do it," Grenyard growled. He extended the flame towards Todd. Horrified, and overcome with grief, the boy shook his head.

"Oswald wouldn't stand for this!" Rob protested.

"Oswald is gone!" Grenyard snapped.

"Please don't!" a Merithian cried, who was no older than Carla. He looked at Todd, as if he knew they shared the same blood. Todd's thoughts screamed, 'Why should he die because of me? Why should any of them die?' Finally, Grenyard lowered his temper.

"You're weak... like your brother... You shall match his fate," Grenyard hissed, causing the Sabre Squadron to seethe. Abbey buried her head in Lanoch's chest, so Grenyard grabbed her chin and forced her to watch, as he tossed his torch on the sailors. An inferno spread across their entangled bodies. Abbey let out a chilling scream. Several prisoners tried to stand, but they were hindered by those bound in agony. A smile stretched across Grenyard's face, as he watched the monstrosity struggle and shriek. Abbey continued screaming as two sailors, wrapped in flames, carried their brothers overboard. The molten tumour hit the icy depths.

"Weak. I'll not suffer frailty!" Grenyard declared, as Abbey delved back into Lanoch's chest.

"Enough!" he shouted. Todd wiped his eyes, whilst trying not to hyperventilate. The smell of burnt flesh resided in their nostrils. Fortunately, their callous leader made his way up onto the quarter deck, so he could address his unit. A backdrop of rotten clouds bled into his attire. Rias appeared behind him, as if he had been whispering in his ear.

"The man's a revenant[27]," Smudge muttered in horror, as Grenyard began speaking.

"The waves swell with Merithian blood. Vaasa, the whole of Scavana, will feel the might of our banner. They set sail to dent our kingdom. Instead, we've fractured their realm. And soon... we shall destroy it." Lieutenant Crawford turned to face his master. A line of corpses lay behind him.

"Don't fret, lieutenant. Victor Skarsgard can keep his bounty and his pathetic, white, ship. This skirmish revealed those who're not worthy of the Skua title. Commit them to the depths. We sail west!" The Sabres scowled in suffering, anger, and confusion. 'West' meant the sands of Sundrith.

***

A melody of hooves carried Don, Laith and Niamh through Cadbey's heartlands. Hills flowed beyond the crinkled leaves and twisted branches. An autumn carpet hid the track. Dry

---

[27] An animated corpse revived from death to haunt the living.

stone walls, layered in moss, kept the riders on a linear path, and a golden brook trickled nearby.

"So, what do you suppose Eldrid and Arthur are planning?" Laith asked, as the cold bit his skin.

A woollen cloak tried to keep him warm. His leather armour had been tested and its studs were rusted. Holsters and satchels hugged his body. His pale horse snorted, as further bags jostled against its sides.

"I'd rather not know," Niamh declared from behind her cowl, whilst smoking a pipe.

Black, studded pads and straps protected her frame. Knives peered from several belts. Crimson boots and gauntlets blended with her stallion's coat.

"It's obvious," said Don. "They're plotting to replace Sartorius with Witherow. Only then can he bring Todd home." They trotted through a stream, where silverfish evaded splashing hooves.

Don's poncho had been conscripted once more. His bones ached from travel and his boots barely fit in the stirrups. And years had passed since he had ridden beyond the outer moors. But only a fool would challenge the three rangers, who rode with conviction.

"Why doesn't the king just appoint Witherow and save us the agro, instead of pardoning him to the mines?" Niamh replied.

"The sorry bastard defied Winsford's law... Besides, it's the king's advisors, more his ministers who hold the power. They decide who stands and who falls. Alan was lucky the advisory intervened at all," Laith explained.

"Niamh's right. They should have appointed Witherow when they had the chance. But I imagine several council members will need removing before Witherow becomes admiral. Not just Sartorius. Revolution or no revolution, I feel a great change is upon us," said Don.

Arthur had fought hard to overturn Alan's untimely sentence. He had gone above Sartorius, to the king and his advisory, who had forced a compromise. Fortunately, the admiral's reputation had been dwindling for decades. Under his poisoned watch, the Skuas had become villains. He had acted desperately to appease the corrupt lords, by weakening the church, and by choosing to provide a slave-force to mine red rock, since they were unable to resettle citizens in Arca. Red rock would give the lords more power. But Sartorius had not questioned whether he would exist in their world. He had angered the council, and republican lords, who suspected the Skuas of killing Johnathan Ackerley. Resilient, Sartorius would use hycinthium-lapis to strengthen his unit and his position, in the name of the king. But the lords were moving faster than he could envisage.

"Treachery is certainly afoot. No one's declared who was behind the drone bombings," said Niamh.

"My money's on the republicans," said Don.

"I wouldn't be so sure," Niamh muttered.

"Let's stay focused. We're only a day's ride ahead of Witherow. We should pick up the pace," Laith suggested.

Alan was bundled into a reinforced carriage, destined for Fort Dry Cote. He would then be taken to Red Rock Citadel. Finally, he would be transferred to the mines of Vanth and Nadym, otherwise known as Dead Man's Chasm. Crowds gathered to observe his exile. Some soldiers greeted him with sympathy and respect. Others despised his tarnished reputation. Alan peered through the barred window of his transport. Ice cracked beneath its wheels, as they left Isabella's Square and the shadow of her statue. They passed through the citadel gates and down into the industrial sector. Hundreds had congregated around Cadbey Central rail station. But their carriage pulled east towards the harbour. A steam engine was left stationary, without fire in its belly.

"Are we not riding the Arca express?" Alan complained. His handcuffs were heavy, the chains between his legs clinked, but his spirit was unbreakable. Two guards tried to ignore him.

The younger guard was called Drew Whittaker. A handlebar moustache curled above his gaunt cheeks. His auburn eyes lacked charisma, but they were focused. Three stripes, on his left arm, meant he was a sergeant. Both men were decked in medals.

"Where did you earn your decorations?" Alan queried. The guards paid him no attention. "Look here lads, if we're travelling by road, a bit of polite conversation wouldn't go amiss."

"You wouldn't know the battle... You've spent too much time at sea," Drew replied. His Arcan accent came from a region known as the black country, named after its abundance of coal. Curious, he clamped his teeth around an obsidian smoking pipe.

"Try me," Alan muttered. He leant forward and offered his ear. Drew pointed to a star on his left breast, which featured a roaring bear.

"I earnt this for my part in the battle of Porth Trefilian[28]."

Many Artayan's[29] believed Cadbey had become a ruling parasite. So, a rebel army had fortified its borders, and bear infested forests, severing Artaya from the realm. Inevitably, Bestla was ordered to remove them. Entire woodlands were incinerated. Bestla's men fought amongst the infernos of hell to bring Artaya under control. They chatted about the conflict and its ferocity. The battle of Porth Trefilian saw the end of the war.

"So... why're we not taking the train, or has my destination changed?" Alan asked. Armed horsemen passed his window, as they traversed the dockyard.

---

[28] The Artayan port city of Trefilian was blockaded, and thousands of fleeing rebels were surrounded and massacred.
[29] Artaya is the Kingdom of Cape Cadbey's most eastern province – a land of rolling hills and ancient woodlands, which line its borders.

"Our destination remains the same. A drone bomb has sabotaged Betton station. The line is out of action," Drew replied, so his older comrade broke his silence.

"Why don't you just un-cuff him whilst you're at it? Tell him where to get off?"

"It's just a little polite conversation," Drew stated. "Anyway, he's not goin' anywhere." Drew respected the ex-vice admiral. He had read about his feats at sea, his calls for reform, and he felt Alan's imprisonment was unjustified. He admired Alan for challenging Winsford's law.

"Mind if I have a toke?" Alan asked. Drew obliged, which made his comrade huff. He placed his pipe in Alan's mouth, who inhaled a large sweep of tobacco, before contemplating Betton. Drone bombs had been used for the first time to incite fear in the capital. Now, Betton had been attacked using the same method.

"I trust Bestla has his best men on the case?" Alan asked.

The older soldier replied, "We all know it's the republicans. Bastards and traitors to the crown. Every one of them should hang!"

"Maybe so," said Alan. "But why would they attack Betton of all places?" Their carriage bumped and juddered, as they exited the docklands and climbed a hill.

"Why betray the king at all? He's a fair king. The fairest this land has seen for centuries, some might say. He gives the lords too much power," said Drew. Alan pondered. He could see the flames of Zora's Lighthouse. Swathes of grass bowed beneath the towering inferno where Todd and his brother would often play, following rare family picnics: first with Martha, then with Viveca. The Aeternum Ocean lay beyond it. As they departed Cadbey, Alan prayed for his son, the realm, and his own safety.

***

Todd's mind had aged a decade. His bones ached, anguish squeezed his brain, but he would heal. The dead, including Carla and Jared, had been wrapped, commemorated, and sent overboard to be claimed by the sea, as they journeyed to Sundrith. Ness, Todd, and Abbey were forced to hold their tears should Grenyard retaliate.

"No frailty," he had growled during a brief funeral, led by a remorseful Lieutenant Crawford. The Sabres had been bound in blood and grief.

The Islet of Winsford failed to distract Todd, as they sailed past its barren terrain. He had dreamt of seeing the island where the Skua legend had been born, but the rock looked soulless. Maybe the story was a lie. Todd had come to realise, all too well, that war was not a fairy-tale. He and Abbey had been left awestruck when they had first boarded the mothership. Now, he realised no one was safe, regardless of age, will or experience. Carla had been in the wrong place at the wrong time. Any Skua could mirror her fate, including Todd, who had barely escaped death.

Their ship skirted north around the Sea of Torment. Cataclysmic maelstroms and tornadoes howled in the distance. This vicious sea had claimed many lives, making the sailors question their destination.

"I tell ye, trouble's brewin'!" said Lanoch. He restrained a cannon, which reflected the crimson lamps.

"Do you think Oswald's in Sundrith?" Rob asked. "He went missing the night we raided Thindraka. He couldn't have gone far." Rob paused in remembrance of his friend Tom Witherow.

"I don't see why we'd risk the Sea of Torment if he wasn't," said Lanoch. "But my gut tells me he's elsewhere. And a Silvashire man always relies on his gut. An' I don't trust Grenyard."

"You and me both. He's a tyrant. He's the reason Jared perished. We'll be lost without him if Sundrith's our destination." Jared had saved them from Sundrith's heartless deserts, callous warriors, and toxic nature. But no more.

"And Carla," Todd muttered.

"Aye," Lanoch nodded. "And wee brave Carla." They wondered what Todd would do if he knew Grenyard's role in his brother's demise. Their assault on Thindraka had been a suicide mission, and Grenyard had orchestrated the operation.

"I hate him," said Todd. Rob comforted the boy, as lightning revealed the event horizon of a distant tornado.

"Careful, Todd. Grenyard is still your commander," Rob stated. Todd frowned at their hypocrisy.

"Bad leaders come n' go, lad. Like the rising and falling of the tide. Just you wait 'n see," Lanoch explained. Todd was infected with a burning ambition. He longed for control, so he could do good in the world. Even if it meant killing the crooked and wicked. Frustrated, Todd made for the barracks.

"I should have stepped in. I should have protected him," said Rob.

"And risk bein' shot by Rias or one of his thugs, then where would the wee boy be, eh?" said Lanoch. His comrade huffed in agreement.

"Grenyard said there's no room for frailty. Yet he punishes the lad for braving the waves, and bleeding alongside his squad-"

"Aye, the man's a lunatic. God knows he shouldn't be at the helm. But we must weather the storm. Pray we find Oswald." The two sailors finished their duties, before finding a place to sleep.

Todd seethed that night, whilst Abbey slept below him. His brother had died and his father had been imprisoned; under Grenyard's command. Now, Carla and Jared lay at the bottom of the ocean, alongside countless other souls, due to Grenyard's blood lust. Furthermore, he and Abbey had been forced to watch prisoners burn. Abbey released a sniffle. Her eyes were fixed on Carla's empty hammock.

"It wasn't your fault," Todd whispered.

"Oh, but it was," Neal replied through the darkness. "I witnessed their frailty when the cannons did roar... Both should have perished."

"Don't listen to him," Todd told Abbey, whose anger began to replace sorrow.

"Like Grenyard said, unworthy of the Skua title," Neal hissed. Todd and Abbey ignored him and nestled into their beds. The boy swore that one day, Grenyard and his followers would pay.

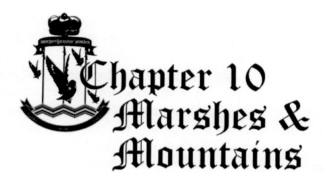

Chapter 10
Marshes &
Mountains

Arcaya may have been conquered centuries ago, but there were still many threats to be feared, such as rebels, highwaymen, wild beasts, and tundra. Don, Niamh and Laith waded through Multa's[30] endless crop yields; and into Arca province, where night was fast approaching. Arca was cold and unforgiving. But they could see Fort Dry Cote, stacked upon a mound. Torches lined its walls and turrets, which towered above a rugged land. Shrines lit a track, otherwise cloaked in darkness. It stretched into the distance, where the Abalone Mountains formed a jagged skyline. Stars glimmered above its impenetrable blackness.

"The fort can wait. We'll observe it in the morning. Let's head back into the forest," Laith suggested. Each adventurer lit a torch, so they could navigate the labyrinth. They soon came across a mysterious ruin, where the forest was still. Nothing stirred in the frost.

"What is it?" Don asked, as their horses circled. Their torches sneered, and sticks snapped beneath restless hooves. Laith looked up to see dozens of bird traps, dangling from the branches.

"An ancient dark force lived here. A witch of sorts – a Veleth. We'll sleep here tonight." Niamh did not believe in such myths, but Don's blood turned cold.

---

[30] Multa is a midland province known for its bountiful harvests.

"No way! I'm not messing about with any dark forces."

"Stop your whining. The old powers have long departed these lands. Yet, others would never dare set foot here. This is where we sleep," Laith demanded. Aching, tired, and hungry; the wanderers set up camp. Timeless, stone pillars surrounded them. Their carvings had been eroded by time, but someone or something had crafted the layer. Don created a campfire, so Niamh could prepare a hare they had hunted along the way. Huge ears drooped from the dog sized beast. Pine tea warmed their stomachs and calmed their nerves. Blankets fended off winter, so they could think of home. Then, the smell of grilled meat stole their senses.

Niamh's teeth pulled at a limb, but this did not stop her from talking.

"Come on then, Laith. What can you tell us about these ancient witches?" Don looked up in frustration, giving Niamh great pleasure. 'How can such a giant be afraid of ghosts?' she thought. Laith sipped his tea and caressed the decorative carvings flattened by eons.

"Some say the Veleths were dictators of fate. Malevolent beings that manipulate men to restore balance in the world. Dark entities that have poisoned kingdoms and ended reigns."

"Bollocks," said Don. He scanned the shadows around them.

Niamh scoffed and asked, "Have you ever come across any?" She smeared her mouth with the back of her hand.

"No," Laith replied. "But there's talk of a Veleth... in the southern Sundrith isles. A dark area untouched by man."

Don moaned, "In all our travels we've never come across any witches, or demons, or malevolent beings. It's bloody crap and you've rambled on about this rubbish before."

Niamh laughed and said, "Keep your toys in your pram. Remind us Laith, what's the name of this she-demon?" Laith leant forward and secured their attention.

"Just whispering her name can bring death… Malkoveleth." A shrill lifted the leaves and caused Don to shiver. Even Laith and Niamh looked startled.

"You bastards," Don moaned. Laith smiled, but he did not want to downplay his people and their beliefs.

"There're many things in this world we do not understand. Powers that are far older than we can conceive," he explained. Satisfied, Niamh changed the topic. Her fox-tail hair was visible in the firelight.

"Where do you suppose our sprogs are?"

"Who knows," said Don. "Probably some distant citadel the world has never heard of."

"I fear for them. It's worse having been there; knowing what they're going through. Mothers of the Oborian Guard can sleep easy," said Niamh.

"Ignorance is bliss," said Laith.

"That same ignorance has made us the villains. The people have no idea what it takes to rule the seas, how much must be sacrificed, and what would happen If we didn't," Don explained.

"…The unit has lost its way. And the world is changing. Maybe there's no need for people like us anymore. All we've ever known is war and bloodshed," said Laith, before tossing a bone into the shadows behind him.

Don concluded, "There'll always be a need for people like us…" The veterans quit their bickering and consoled each other. They retreated under their bivvies[31] and focused on their mission. Niamh hummed a song to comfort them.

"Light of the moon and Zora's Star
Show me the way, to lands afar
Keep me safe when the cannons do roar
I pray to you, Zora's star"

---

[31] A simple diagonal shelter used to sleep under.

***

Don awoke instantly. His brain would trick him into thinking Death was near. Sunlight flickered through a thicket of branches. Rain patted his face and wintered leaves. Further droplets pelted a tin-box with musical precision. Reassured, the ogre pulled his blanket over his face to rid the world. Crackling thunder tormented him. Then, a second unnatural rumble grabbed his attention. Niamh burst from her sleeping sack.

"That's gunfire!" she blurted. Her hair was wild and furious. Shocked, they grabbed their weapons and hurried towards the tree line with their horses in tow.

Rain was draped over the battlefield. Frozen peaks formed a phenomenal backdrop. Cannons shelled Fort Dry Cote from the north. Muzzle-flash revealed militants, as they pressed through the gloomy mire. Niamh suggested it was the Ebony Knights, merciless rebels from Ebonshire. They would cross into Arca, to attack wealthy outposts and settlements. A cannon ball smashed the fortress! The garrison returned fire, as brick tumbled into the shadows. The veterans absorbed a nostalgic dose of chaos. Horns raised the alarm, screams echoed through the valley, explosions lit their eyes, but their amazement was short lived. A group of messengers escaped south on horseback, and a flock of carrier pigeons were released into the air.

"Well, that's soddin' brilliant!" Niamh shouted. "There's no way Witherow's convoy will stop at the garrison now!" Laith studied the battlefield, as rain spilled down their faces.

"We'll have to head back. We'll cut around the fort to the south. The convoy will still have to pass through the Abalone Mountains," he explained. Don shook his sopping head.

"The land to the south is filled with moon marshes. We'd have to abandon the horses. We'd never make it in time - that's if we don't drown in the process!" Their cloaks soaked up the storm. A carrier pigeon disappeared over the trees behind them.

"We don't have a choice!" Laith argued. "Our northern route is compromised, and reinforcements will be on the way. We head southwest."

"Can't we ambush the convoy before it reaches the garrison?" Don argued.

"No… Laith's right. We don't have a choice. Let's move out," said Niamh. Don huffed, before following their lead. They were right. No other location would allow them to accomplish such a daring rescue.

They retraced hoof prints, exited the forest, and orbited around its mass. Fort Dry Cote endured to the north, where towers of smoke stood over the land. The onslaught had faded, but the rain persisted. Laith insisted they abandon the road, as they were insight of the military bastion. Shivering, the Skuas followed a trail west, until their path disappeared into a bog. Nature had reclaimed the track and any shrines built beside it. Their horses grew wary of its treacherous slides and perilous pits, which exhaled the stench of rot.

"This is where we leave the horses," said Niamh, who could not bear to see her steeds suffer. They dismounted and gathered anything they could carry.

"This is suicide!" Don shouted, as he felt his weight increase by fifty pounds. Determined, Niamh sent their horses away. Their owners persevered into an unforgiving marshland.

Clumps of sod ushered their feet into the depths of a forbidden land. Icy waters filled their boots. Contorted trees tried to help, but their branches were too brittle. Then, Don slipped and screamed, as he became submerged in a corpse. Bloated flesh and distorted features revolved in the murky pond.

"Don't just stand there, help me!" Don shouted, as the carcase invaded his space. Laith hurried over. He dragged his friend onto a slab of moss, situated beside the waterlogged grave.

"Who's your new friend?" Niamh asked from a standing position, which caused Don to curse.

"He must have been a prisoner, who fled Fort Dry Cote. The marshes are full of them," Laith said, panting. Their bodies were caked in mud. The sky showed no mercy, as the rain poured down. Blades of grass, thorns and thistles surrounded them, like a thousand knives encrusted in jewels.

"Skuas don't belong on land, and this is why. It's horrible. Mud and bones and bastard camping," Don shouted.

"Shut up," Niamh barked. "We've still got that bastard mountain to climb, or we'll never intercept the convoy!" A hideous facade of rock and snow could be seen in the distance. Sleet veiled its dreadful face. The travellers composed themselves, clambered to their feet, and powered on. But their thoughts became frantic, as the sun began to set. They could not navigate the moon marshes at night. Their troubled minds wandered, until a strange, mechanical noise grasped their attention. Then, two steel jaws snapped shut. Niamh let out a blood curdling scream. Don splashed through the marsh towards her. Her leg stood twisted in the clutches of a beartrap! Laith kept Niamh standing, whilst Don wrapped his hands around the mechanism. The giant growled, as he pulled the contraption open, but he could not hold it. The teeth snapped shut again!

"BASTARD!" Niamh wailed. Blood streamed from her chewed boot. "I don't want to die here."

"Shut up, we're getting you out of here!" Don shouted. He grabbed the vile machine for a second time, but he could not best its jaws, so Niamh pleaded for him to stop. The falling sun crushed their spirits. A mist crept in to smother their hope. Her emerald eyes begged for freedom, as she braced for another attempt. Then, a torch appeared through the fog.

"Who goes there!?" came a loud voice. Laith reached for his revolver, but his fingers were swollen beyond use.

Shaking, Don revealed his blade, but his limbs were restrained by bog. Just as they were about to despair, another voice suggested they were rebels.

"Ebony knights, sheath your arms. You're safe now," the torch bearer shouted. The veterans stayed silent, as a group of nomads came to their aid.

Their furs made them look like demons of the mire. Torches hissed in the rain. Their leader knelt beside Niamh. A heavy, wolf pelt concealed his head. Its teeth glinted in the firelight. A robust beard emphasised his jaw line. His fur boots, clothes and mittens stunk of bog. A rifle remained fixed to his back, as he examined the fused beartrap. The handle of a silver battle axe protruded from his hip.

"Well, well, what do we have here? A mark three beartrap, most likely left for me and my men!" said the stranger. "But just like the mark two, its spring can be removed in a jiffy!" Laith watched in apprehension, as the hunter dismantled the trap. Niamh passed out, so Laith lay her down in the moss. He cut the boot from her shin, before applying a bandage yanked from his kit bag. "Don't worry. We'll get your friend fixed up. I'm Erus by the way." The werewolf extended his hand; but Laith, wary and preoccupied, refused his gesture. Instead, he gave the wolf his name.

Unoffended, the nomad replied, "Laith... that's a Sundrithian name. Don't worry, we've got a few Sundrithians amongst our ranks. Even a few Merithians…"

"Merithians?" Don asked. Witherow may have taken a Merithian bride, but this had been excused by his clan. They had never seen Viveca as a threat, for she had treated their wounds and shown nothing but compassion.

"We share common ground. The enemy of my enemy is my friend and all that malarkey. Come on, let's get your friend out of this piss basin!" Don placed Niamh over his shoulders like a child. Then, they proceeded through the marsh. Erus knew the everglade and all its secrets.

A howling wind chilled their bones. Torches caused withered trees to flicker from their periphery. Rain turned to sleet, and sleet turned to snow, as the path became steep and gravelled. They had reached the Abalone Mountains.

"How much further?" Don pleaded. Erus assured them there was a cave up ahead. The veterans were dubious, but Erus delivered on his promise.

They entered a sanctuary. A flame was tossed onto a central firepit, creating a bed of hot coals. Flickering tongues revealed a hive of stamped crates, stolen equipment, barrels and sleeping sacks. Torn flags and ripped sheets hid damp rock. Erus snapped an icicle from the ceiling and commanded his men to prepare food for their guests. Drained, Don set Niamh down near the fire, so Laith could tend to her wounds. Miraculously, her leg remained unbroken.

"Lucky, her shin must have slipped between the teeth!" said Don.

"Describe this as lucky one more time. I dare you," Niamh huffed as she awoke. She extended her hand, so Don passed her a flask of whisky to numb the pain. The werewolf loomed over them with an offering: cheese, bread, and a canteen of water, with an icicle sticking out of the top.

"She'll be right as rain in no time. You boys fought hard today... and the lady of course," said Erus. He perched himself on a crate beside them and removed his pelt, to reveal a mane of lustrous, black hair. His broad face encased two cobalt eyes, which desired trust, but he was a rebel and a thief. "What was it like out there? Did you breach the fort?" Don paused in thought. He could swear he recognised the mountain dweller. Laith was too honest to answer. Fortunately, Niamh still had air in her lungs.

"We were hoping you could tell us... we were sent south on a flanking mission... But we were spotted and ambushed; forced deeper into the marsh." The wolf took a bite from his apple, before continuing his interrogation.

"Aggus sends three soldiers on a flanking mission. Strange. And where's your armour?" He smeared the juice from his beard. The Ebony Knights were known for wearing armour plating, reclaimed from a bygone era. It was meant to reflect their honour and skill in battle, and their right to rule over Ebonshire. Don stated they had ditched their cumbersome gear. And he assured Erus that they had been far greater in number, before the ambush had occurred.

"Well, I hope there's no hard feelings. We would've come sooner. But general Aggus, as he so arrogantly calls himself, refuses to pay, so he'll receive no further help from us. You're lucky we ventured out at all," Erus explained. 'No honour among thieves,' Don thought.

Peter Aggus had led the Ebony Knights through decades of strain. They had been decommissioned by the crown, who deemed their code nonprogressive. Furthermore, the monarchy had appointed Lady Jillian Devon to rule. Exiled to the Feral Pits[32], Peter's forces longed for independence, but they could not survive without capturing resources from Arca. This meant seeking the help of Erus and his Abalone Guerrillas, who demanded payment for safe passage through the mountains. Their nomadic ways had also been rejected by the crown. The clans of Abalone had refused to pledge their allegiance to King Oborus II, resulting in several massacres. But Bestla had underestimated their strength. He refused to believe they were anything more than a band of vagabonds. He was confident the Oborian Guard would succeed, as it had done in Artaya.

"Say, I noticed when you were cutting your friend's boot off that you have a Skua blade," said Erus. "Now, where in hell did you find one of those?" The wolf leant forward and licked his lips.

---

[32] A hostile ravine in Ebonshire inhabited by predators and bone yards.

"Does it matter?" said Laith. Erus was tired and hungry, and decided to question them no further. His game was to be continued.

"Tonight, we feast, rest... sadly there's nothing to screw. And in the morning, we'll fly a message to Aggus, to let him know you're here. How's about that?" Erus clapped his hands and disappeared into the cave. The veterans gulped a cup of unease. Niamh needed time to heal, but the Ebony Knights would expose them, unless Erus could beat them to it. Don gazed at the cave's exit. The Abalone Mountains were merciless. Niamh would surely die amongst the ice if they tried to leave. Then, there was the mission to consider.

"He looks familiar," Don whispered.

"Don't all heathens?" Laith replied, whilst tightening Niamh's bandages.

"What are we gonna do?"

"For now, we tend to Niamh and try and get some rest. We'll need it." A few rebels sang, whilst drinking whisky by the fire.

"The clans who thrived in high Abalone
Would not pledge allegiance, to Cadbey's throne
So they cut the clans down in the midst of night
For giving them ale, respect, and respite"

"I prefer Niamh's singing," Don muttered.

Both Don and Laith fought to stay awake. But exhaustion forced their eyes to close. Shadows danced. The fire bed crackled. Embers kept the whistling wind from entering their hollow, deep within the Abalone Mountains.

Chapter 11
The Scathed
Sickle Pass

Don awoke to see Erus standing over him like a tombstone. He clasped his battle axe, which had slain many foes.

"Wake up you big bastard… We've got lamb chops and eggs for breakfast!" Don sat up and shook Laith awake. Niamh remained asleep next to the fire bed.

"Do you treat all your guests this well?" Don asked.

"Only those who're prepared to fight," said Erus with a grin. He leaned his axe against a crate, which made Don feel more at ease.

"How long will you fight?" he asked. The mud on his clothes had formed a crust.

"I'll die fighting," Erus said with pride. "Oborus wants all the riches in these mountains and beyond. But he doesn't want us or our culture. He doesn't understand that these peaks are sacred. That they belong to us. We're the true peoples of Arca. And you're the true knights of Ebonshire, no?" Don yawned to buy himself time, so Laith posed a question.

"Forgive me, but you don't sound like you were born on the mountain." He removed a canteen so he could wet his mouth. Erus admired his awareness and grinned once more.

"My ancestors were nomads. I've simply returned to fight the good fight." Don nor Laith believed the wolf. Many had joined the Abalone Guerrillas, the Ebony Knights, or similar factions, because they were running from their past. A snow dusted guerrilla approached them with news.

"Erus, there's a convoy on route to the south. It'll pass straight through the sickle!"

The Scathed Sickle Pass was named after it cursed shape. Its layout was perfect for an ambush. Travellers were unable to see around its bend, and its narrow ends could be blocked. Laith assumed the guerrilla meant Witherow's convoy. Erus patted his comrade on the arm before suggesting he eat.

"Right, it's time you boys made yourselves useful," said the wolf, before wandering over to the fire. Several clay pots had been surrounded by ashes, and chunks of meat were sizzling in their confines. The veterans had been left hanging, so Don questioned their mission.

"Good, so you're keen! It's what I like to call a candy snatch. Stop the convoy, loot the convoy, dance around the convoy, and hire any prisoners in the process," Erus explained. "So, you boys in?" Laith and Don glanced at each other, before nodding in acquiescence. "Good, I expected nothing less."

"What of Niamh?" Laith asked. She had yet to wake, and her skin was pale.

"Don't worry, she'll be reunited with your tribe by the time we get back," said Erus. The veterans resisted the urge to panic. The Ebony Knights were on their way. They finished their breakfast with haste. Then, Erus ordered his men to form a parade outside. Everything had been covered in a blanket of snow. Flakes continued to fall from a grey canopy. They could see Fort Dry Cote in the distance between two shallow peaks. The stronghold looked as if it had been built on a sheet of mist, which obscured the moon marshes they had traversed the night before. The forest they had camped in was barely visible. Erus addressed his warriors of ice and fury.

"Men of the mountain. Today we hunt! Our friends from Ebonshire have kindly diverted a convoy towards the Scathed Sickle. Let us seize the day and whatever prize it may carry.

These knights will be joining us. Let's see if we can teach them a thing or two." A pack of eight rebels gave them a dirty look, before setting off through the snow, armed with muskets, hatchets, and knives. Fur boots waded through the frozen tundra. The veterans hung back so they could talk. Frost escaped their lips.

"Remind you of anyone?" Don asked.

"I've been thinking about what you said. He does look familiar," said Laith.

"Not Erus. The situation. Soldiers heading out on a raid, in a bid to protect their homeland?"

"They're enemies of the king. Nothing more." A rebel looked back, which encouraged them to keep up. But Don was reluctant to leave Niamh behind.

"We don't have a choice," said Laith. "We must protect Witherow when they attack." Virgin snow crunched beneath their boots, as they drifted further from their injured friend.

"But the Ebony Knights will expose her... Let me slip away in the snow. I'll head back and make sure she's safe whilst you-"

"No," said Laith. "If you go back, they'll capture you both. We must adapt... Let's use these dogs to our advantage. We'll intercept the convoy and free Witherow. Then we'll plan Niamh's extraction. She's more than capable of handling herself until then. That wounded leg won't hinder her bite." They disappeared through the gentle blizzard.

***

Alan pressed his hands against the ceiling, as their carriage careered over a pothole. Cracking whips caused the horses to neigh. The sun was setting, their stomachs were groaning, a mist was rising, but their convoy showed no signs of stopping. Alan asked why they were in such a hurry.

"We know as much as you," Drew replied calmly.

"Well, stick your 'ead out n' see if anyone's steering this rust bucket!" Alan suggested.

"So be it," said Drew, before finishing his pipe. His older comrade aimed a pistol at Alan, to prevent any tricks. "It's nothing personal," Drew assured. Then, he unlocked the roof hatch and peered out. A crazed driver, in a tri-corn hat and tailcoat, clung to a set of frenzied reigns. Branches zipped past overhead. Drew asked where they were heading.

"Fort Dry Cote has been attacked, so we're taking the southern road. Orders are to ride under the cover of nightfall straight for Red Rock Citadel!" the driver shouted. Drew returned to his seat.

"That'll be the Abalone Guerrillas… and now your commander wishes us ta ride through the lion's den in the hope nightfall will hide this racket?" said Alan. "Can we not turn back?"

"You'd like that wouldn't ya," said the older guard.

"You better make sure your bayonets are sharper than their axes!" said Alan. The air grew thin, and the mountain drew near.

***

Embers caused the air to blur. Niamh realised a sinister nomad was watching her through the haze, whilst picking meat from his teeth. His gaunt face was smothered in dirt. Greasy strands of hair tried to hide his offensive looks and bulging eyes.

"How's the leg?" he asked in a grim voice.

"Piss off," said Niamh. She gripped her blade beneath her blanket. The bony figure stood up and walked towards a boiling pot of grog. He spoke in a hollow voice, as he ladled the harsh brew.

"I first came across the Ebony Knights when I was just a boy. I was staying in a village inn with my parents." The man was named Nester. He barely flinched, as he sipped the strong liquor. "The Knights had a disagreement with the landlord and decided they would treat the house as their own." Niamh lacked patience. She had silenced many swines, but her injury beseeched caution, so she listened. "They ransacked the inn. I remember the screams from the bar downstairs... as they stabbed and slashed without mercy. Worse... I remember the cries my mother made, after my father was no longer able to protect her. And once the knights had finished... I remember the flames... as my eyes remained fixed on their remains..." Nester glared at Niamh.

"Erus!" a voice bellowed. Nester jumped from his skin, as another call boomed through the cave. A group of seven wanderers trudged into view. Black breastplates and spaudlers glinted in the firelight; the Ebony Knights had arrived. Some wore terrifying visors from a bygone era. Metallic skulls covered their faces, iron fangs drooled molten snow, horns grazed the ceiling, and their capes swept the floor. Each soldier wielded a shotgun, but some carried maces or axes. Their leader flung his visor open to reveal a beaten face and stern, gun-metal eyes.

"Aggus!" Nester stuttered. Niamh shrunk into her sleeping sack and pretended to be asleep.

"Give me a bastard drink!" the war-torn knight demanded. Trembling, Nester abandoned his resentment and poured the man a cup of grog. Aggus snatched the beverage from his hand and gulped the fiery liquid. "Help yourselves men!" His band began scavenging supplies.

"You can't take everything. It's not yours!" said Nester.

"I don't believe it's yours either," Aggus replied. Everything had been stolen from nearby settlements or convoys. He stepped towards the rat, which caused his armour to clink. "My men are fresh from the field of battle; something you wouldn't recognise, because you hide in the mountains, whilst we bleed at castle walls!"

"Erus will be back soon," Nester declared.

"And I shall be gone. Now where are my men?" Nester admitted his knights had joined Erus on a skirmish. The general's frown deepened.

"But there's one down there, under those pelts," Nester stuttered. Aggus made his way over to Niamh's blanket and pulled it back!

***

Don, Laith, Erus and his pack had pushed southwest through the mountains. The air felt vacuous. Night would soon be upon them, and temperatures well below freezing. They reached the Scathed Sickle Pass before hiking north towards the ambush zone. Stone teeth overhung the disfigured passage. The road below was flooded with darkness. It was more of a natural gorge then a manmade path. The full moon peered over a mountain top, and its rays caused the snow to glow.

"I don't know how they survive out here. I really don't," Don's teeth chattered.

"War keeps their hearts warm," said Laith. Suddenly, a grey horse cantered past them. Its scout wore furs that offered camouflage and protection.

"You're not going to believe this," the white rider told Erus. "The prisoner cargo is Alan Witherow." The wolf froze.

"Thee Witherow. As in the vice admiral?" Erus questioned.

"A runner from Cadbey reached our camp this morning. I set out as soon as I could." Erus thanked the rider and insisted he eat. The veterans carefully approached him.

"An old friend of yours?" Don asked. Flakes nested in his beard and settled upon his cape.

Erus shook his head and grunted, "Nare!" The wolf gathered his men. The atmosphere changed along with his demeanour.

"Change of plan," Erus shouted. "Alan Witherow approaches in chains. I want him alive... So I can carve out his tongue and feed it to him!" Don swore under his breath. They could no longer use the Abalone Guerrillas to their advantage. Every step brought them closer to their friend's demise. They desperately tried to understand who Erus was, and why he wanted Alan dead.

"I remember," said Laith. He was forced to pause as a rebel overtook them. "I'm sure it's him."

"Who!?" Don urged.

"He was on the same ship we found Viveca. In the Sea of Forts. But his name isn't Erus." Don suddenly twigged.

"Rorik," he muttered. "His name is Rorik." The dissident had hinted at his origins, before rescuing them from the marshes.

Rorik was a Merithian marine. Over a decade had passed since the Skuas had captured Rorik, Viveca, and their crew. Viveca had agreed to heal the wounded. But Rorik would not yield. He had fallen for Viveca, whilst a patient in her care. It pained him to see her fraternize with the enemy, and he could sense Alan's feelings towards her. The bitter sting of jealously convinced him that she had been enslaved, so the Merithian developed a lust for vengeance. Enraged, he mutilated several Skuas before trying to escape. Alan punished him severely. His body still bore the scars. Rorik was sentenced to death, but the relentless brute had escaped and fled into the mountains.

"What are we supposed to do now?" Don asked. His thighs burned from trudging through snow, and he could no longer feel his feet. "What if he recognises us. What if this is all a game!" Rorik had questioned Laith's Skua blade.

"Everything alright back there?" One of Rorik's thugs had noticed their wittering. The veterans nodded and waited until their foe was distracted.

"We must protect Witherow at all costs. Go, take Niamh and head for Red Rock Citadel. I will distract these scum long enough for the convoy to pass," Laith ordered, but Don fervently defied him. "It was *you* who suggested sneaking away in the snow. And that's what you must do. You *must* rescue Niamh so Alan can walk free another day. It's the only way," the warrior explained. They were running out of time. Rorik's men had begun their preparations. Heaps of rock would be sent downhill to block the passage and cripple the convoy.

"No," Don blurted. He could not stand the thought of leaving Laith. A foreboding fog gate lingered behind him.

"What happens if we both fall? What will become of Niamh or Alan?" Laith argued. His comrade dropped his head. "Don't worry about me, brother. I was born from ash, a land full of peril. Yet, I'm still here. We'll link up in Red Rock Citadel. Now go!" Laith pulled their foreheads together.

"Take my blade," Don insisted. "I've seen what you can do with two of these." He handed him his Skua dagger. "I want it back." Laith made no promises, as the large sailor faded into a steady snowfall.

Laith could sense Death's presence. The marine knelt in the frost and observed his surroundings. Nine entities, including the white rider, had fortified the upper gorge. Two militants were stood on a ridge to his left. The others were situated off to his right, where the boulders had been set. Laith would assault them long enough for the convoy to pass. Then he would make his getaway. The ravine offered protection if he could stick to the shadows. But ominous shapes lingered in the darkness. Any one of them could be his downfall. The Abalone Guerrillas were known for fighting up close, and the five bullets in his revolver would not be enough to stop an advance. They would charge him with fearsome weapons designed to hack, slash, and dismember their victims. A perilous edge offered its allegiance; the guerrillas would have less poise on its slick surface, yet the odds were against him. His cold joints ached, and the snow would do its best to restrain him. Suddenly, the pass began to rumble, hooves could be heard in the distance. Rorik ordered his men into position. Laith rose to his feet, withdrew his revolver, and unsheathed his blade. But something far more sinister was lurking in the shadows…

As he stepped forth, a rebel yelped, followed by a yowl, which echoed through the valley. Laith pivoted to see a snow leopard, wrapped around a guerrilla. Paws tore at his body and teeth imbedded his face. The two militias in front of Laith turned, so the veteran rushed the nearest guerrilla, who failed to trigger his rifle. Laith parried the gun, pistol whipped his foe, and swiped upward with his blade! The rebel's neck split open like a ruptured eel, then he plummeted off the ravine. Laith ducked as the second man fired! The blast ripped a hole in his cape, but the veteran was left unharmed. He launched his dagger, which pierced the nomad's head. Vanquished, his target collapsed in the snow. No longer crisp, its crumpled sheet turned black, as if it had been infected. Laith tugged his knife from a fractured skull. The Sundrithian warrior flicked his weapon clean and set his sights on the leopard. The beast was sparring with a rebel, so three onlookers turned their attention to Laith, whilst another tried to dislodge a boulder with Rorik's assistance. Laith did not hesitate. He extended his revolver and fired all five shots with deadly precision! One bandit slipped on the ice, whilst vomiting guts. The others sprawled to the ground, twitching and bloodied. Rorik was forced to intervene. The wolf abandoned his boulder, swung his axe, and downed the big cat. His men sprung forth to beat the crippled leopard, as Laith tossed his revolver aside, and revealed his second dagger. The clamour of hooves and carriages boomed. Snow tumbled down the mountain! Infuriated, Rorik rushed the boulder, so his remaining fighters could assault Laith with their hatchets. The Sundrithian slashed, dodged and danced with superior agility. Blood lashed the ground, but his enemies persisted. Frozen breath formed a cloud around them, as serrated edges cut flesh from bone. Ultimately, they could stand no more. The nomads fell to their knees, gurgling and crying, and slumped to their faces. To Laith's horror, Rorik had succeeded. Rocks crashed into the passage below. Laith growled, as a carriage exploded beneath the avalanche! But a stream of lanterns slid through the abyss. Laith prayed that Alan was not on-board the obliterated vessel.

"It's over, Rorik!" he shouted. His clothes were dripping in blood. Eight men and a beast lay dead, as the sound of hooves faded into the distance. The moon cast an eerie glow upon the tarnished frost. Glistening flakes tried to repair the damage.

"You sorry prick," Rorik spat. "I was gonna have my wolves gut you and Witherow like pigs."

"I must commend you for your act. You're not a wolf, more a snake."

"I was barely a man when you bastards brought me here. Gaining the lingo was the least of my concerns."

"Why not return to Merithia? You don't belong here," Laith asked, as if their encounter could have been avoided.

"That makes two of us," said Rorik, who had nearly regained his breath.

"Witherow gave me a purpose and saved my son."

"That bastard took everything from me. Everything! My freedom, my crew, my love!" Rorik had let years of anxiety plague him with madness. He had dwelled amongst the mountain: writhing, scathing, and seeking vengeance. Laith's blades glinted in the moonlight. Rorik began looting a mauled corpse, so the veteran began his approach, but as he moved near, Rorik snatched a gun from a lifeless hand. Laith gasped as Rorik aimed and fired, putting a bullet through his torso. The gunshot echoed a dozen times, as Laith dropped to his knees. His wound drooled. It melted the snow below him, as he struggled for air in a heartless place.

"The only good Oborian is a dead Oborian. I'll find Witherow and I'll send the bastard straight to hell, which is exactly where you're heading!" said Rorik. He dropped his pistol and clasped his axe in both hands. The snow crunched as he marched towards Laith. Fretting, desperate, the veteran scrambled towards the edge and threw himself into the gorge!

***

Shaking, Don struggled to lift his legs above a rising tide of snow. The footsteps he had been following had vanished, and he felt lost amongst the Abalone Mountains. Perilous thoughts shrouded his mind, so he pictured his son, Robert.

Rob had always been a smaller version of himself. Although they were both large in stature, Don remained the biggest. He had done his best to prepare Rob for the navy, in line with Winsford's law, so he was confident his son was safe. Pride warmed his heart, as he remembered Rob's thirteenth birthday. The mothership had returned to Cadbey, meaning Don was fortunate enough to come ashore. There was cake, whisky, and an uncontrollable pub crawl, resulting in mischief. They had snuck aboard the mothership, so Rob could gain 'work experience'. But he ended up vomiting in an officer's boot. His mother, Sarah was not impressed when they returned home, far past dawn, but she had married into a sailor's world. Sadly, Sarah had died from consumption two years later, whilst Rob was at sea. Don had returned home to ease her passing. He clutched a gold necklace and its locket, which had belonged to her. But he could barely picture her face, and their shared memories were too scarce. Only Niamh crept into his imagination, and what could have been. Shivering, he thought about Laith's son, Jared; Niamh's daughter, Vanessa; Thomas Witherow, and Todd's newfound burden at such a young age. They had to save Alan, for his sake, if nothing else. So, Don persevered through the blizzard, whilst hoping he would recognise the path.

***

Niamh's face leaked sweat and blood, as she stared into the embers below her. She had been strung up by her wrists, above the crackling fire bed. Flames licked her boots, in a bid to claim their prize. Bandages hid her gruesome leg. Most of the Ebony Knights had fallen asleep, but Aggus remained: prowling, mumbling, and drinking.

He had removed his armour, releasing the stench of war. Grey hair brushed his shoulders and a leather shirt. Necklaces had become tangled in his forested chest. He nudged Niamh awake, which caused her wrists to burn.

"You will tell me who you are before the dawn, or you will burn," Aggus grunted. "Your friends will return to find your body blackened. And then they will burn beside you. Unless you tell me what three Skuas are doing in the Abalone Mountains?" Nester watched from the shadows. A sickness within him enjoyed Niamh's torment. But his resentment for the Ebony Knights had returned. Niamh refused to break, but she could not hold out much longer. Her boot ignited causing her to groan in pain.

"Hurts, doesn't it?" said Aggus. "Imagine that feeling across your entire body." Smoke began to rise, as Niamh tried to wriggle. Her abductor began laughing. Then, he unbuttoned his trousers and urinated on her molten boot. The flames hissed and retreated.

"I once said, I wouldn't piss on an Oborian if they were on fire. Turns out I was wrong," the inebriated ogre chuckled. No one was awake to admire his humour, so his tone changed. "You're lucky. Lucky you're old...useless...dying." Aggus squeezed her thighs and sniffed her leather attire. "If you were a few years younger, we'd have tossed you all around this cave. You'd be begging for the flames... or more. I hear you Skua girls like it rough." Suddenly, a rag appeared in his mouth. Then a sword exited his chest! The blade reversed, only to reappear through his neck. The cloth turned red and prevented Aggus from screaming. Nester's bulbous eyes glowed with vengeance, as the knight slumped to his knees. The rat pushed the ogre into the cinders. Aggus's flesh began to spit and sizzle, as his clothes combusted. Stunned, Niamh tried her best to avoid the spread of flames.

"Get me down," she dribbled. Nester could not watch the Ebony Knights repeat what they had done to his mother. But he did not care for Niamh. She was still the enemy, and Rorik would want his say. Possessed, Nester began slitting the throat of every Ebony Knight. They gurgled and thrashed as they awoke. Blood spurted the contents of their cave. One of the drunken knights arose, grabbed his axe, and embedded it in Nester's side. He cried, before plunging his sword through the knight's stomach. Avenged, Nester collapsed into a puddle of gore, where he was reunited with his parents. The doomed knight staggered through the cave and disappeared into the blizzard.

Aggus's corpse continued to blaze. Niamh whimpered, as she tried to avoid the smell of burnt flesh. Her shins glowed, her bruises pulsed, her gums bled. She begged for Don or Laith to appear, but no one came. Minutes felt like hours. Hours felt like days. Eventually, the fire receded. Bones lay amongst the ashes of a forgotten conflict. Knights lay slain in their armour. Nester remained still, with an axe rooted in his side. Niamh's tomb became dark and cold, and all became silent.

Until a groan echoed through the cavern. Dawn had broken, and Niamh awoke to see a large silhouette stood in the opening. Her vision was blurred, as the figure approached. But a roar heightened her senses. To her horror, a black bear had entered the dwelling. The megalithic beast began sniffing the dead. The bear made its way over to Niamh, who tried not to panic. Its muzzle sniffed the air around her, but it could not stand the charred fire-bed. Niamh fastened her eyes and remained still. Fortunately, the behemoth detected a different scent. Huge paws toppled a blood-splattered crate, to reveal parcels of meat. The creature snorted, as it gorged on the free meal. Exhausted, Niamh continued to fall in and out of consciousness. She opened her eyes, to see the beast had moved. The silhouette had returned to the mouth of the cave. Suddenly, the creature spoke.

"Niamh…" It was Don. He stumbled forth, kicking hot ashes aside, and supported Niamh's weight. His frost-bitten feet could not detect surviving coals, as he accidently hugged her mangled shin.

"Cut me down you prick," Niamh uttered. The ice giant located Nester's sword and freed his friend. He lay her down on the ground.

"Water," she coughed, but Don was one step ahead. He fumbled his canteen into position so she could drink. As Niamh gulped, Don glanced the terrors around them.

"What… happened here?" his blue lips asked.

"Whisky," Niamh demanded, so Don obliged.

"I'm sorry… I took so long... I got lost, in the blizzard… Then, I found the body of an Ebony knight. His footprints led me here… but there was a bear. You wouldn't believe the size of it," Don explained. "The bear must have had its fill. Or it's feasted on that knight." Blood entered Niamh's limbs, causing her wrists to sting. Nothing hurt more than her grilled, chewed leg. Don headed outside and returned with a cape full of snow, so he could sooth Niamh's wounds. Then, he grabbed a rogue piece of loin and placed it against her bruised cheek. Lastly, he reinstated a fire and put further slabs of meat inside a cooking pot, so they could feast.

They rested for a while, as if locked in a trance. Shadows danced across the walls. Finally, Niamh asked about Laith's whereabouts. Don strained to tell her about Rorik and their decision to separate.

"Were Viveca and Rorik ever an item?" Don asked.

"What would I know?" Niamh slurred, as whisky trickled down her chin. "I think we've got bigger issues."

"Women talk," Don shrugged.

"Viveca never mentioned Merithia… or Rorik. She left that world behind. And she was barely in this one five minutes." Viveca was arrested and executed for espionage. Many believed her only crime was being married to a former vice admiral. No one could protect her, not even Alan. Don asked

Niamh if she thought Viveca was a spy. May be Rorik had found her after escaping.

"We've had this discussion before," said Niamh. "I don't know, and I don't care." Niamh was right - they had bigger problems to worry about. The general of the Ebony Knights, Peter Aggus lay cremated at their feet; Niamh was immobile, and Rorik could be on route. They had failed their mission and Alan was on his way to Red Rock Citadel. Still, they failed to stay awake.

The sun was beginning to rise when Don awoke. Propelled by fear, he nudged Niamh awake, causing her wounds to burn. Neither had gained the rest they deserved.

"I'm sorry, Niamh. We must be leaving..."

"Leave me," she murmured.

Don sneered, "You don't mean that."

"I don't... but we don't have a choice," said Niamh. Tears welled in her eyes. Don poked the flames in frustration, until his determination triumphed.

"I've been told that three times since Fort Dry Cote... by you... and Laith. I *do* have a choice. And I'm not leaving you here." Don clambered to his feet. The Abalone Mountains would not best him. He strapped large hooping platforms to his feet, to give him a better footing, and he snatched two walking polls. Then, he took a helmet from an Ebony Knight, to protect him from the breeze. Finally, he dressed Niamh in new bandages and furs.

"Thank you, Don." She placed her feeble hand against his visor.

"It's not the first time we've been in this state," he replied with a smile. He was both glad and sad that she could not see him blush.

"I know... You never let me down." She embraced his hand. "Do you think we'll see our kids again?" she asked in search of inspiration.

"Like Arthur said, Alan's only son is out there. And he's the only one who can bring him home. That means bringing our kids home to."

Niamh sniffled and nodded before saying, "Alright... let's finish this, and bring them home."

Devoted, Don lifted her onto his back. He suggested they try and find Laith at the Scathed Sickle Pass. They left Aggus's crypt behind and ultimately set off for Red Rock Citadel.

Chapter 12
The Greatest Evil

Todd followed the burning sun and twinkling constellations across the heavens, until it was time to dwell again. His knowledge of the world was increasing. His lust for vengeance failed to dampen, especially whilst in the presence of Grenyard, Neal, Rias, and his thugs. The cadets were becoming just as fearsome and astute as their leaders. Rias was sharpening Neal, who had convinced Gregory that Sundrithians and Merithians were inferior. He believed they had infected the unit, making it weak, and that Cadbey needed cleansing. But Sundrithians, like Laith and Jared, had made the unit stronger. Sundrithia produced the finest warriors, whose hand-to-hand fighting techniques had been adopted by the R.B.S. Yet, prejudice had found its voice. Abbey was beginning to adopt Lanoch's accent. Now and then, her tongue would produce a Silvashire tone, which Todd found amusing.

Land appeared in the distance like a mirage. Heat waves beat off its scorched body and hot stones glinted like beacons. They had reached the charred shores of Sundrith. Crawford insisted they sail north, by following a jagged coastline of blackened rock. Lanoch appeared by his side on the quarter deck.

"What will it be, lieutenant? A raiding party? A scout-party? A siege!?" He scoffed a boiled egg, as a sign of disrespect, whilst waiting for a response. His superior seemed more anxious than usual; Crawford could barely look the captain in his eyes. Carla's death had left its mark, but his anxiety was fixated elsewhere.

"No. We go ashore."

"What, the whole ship?" Lanoch asked. Crawford nodded, so the captain joked, "Is this a vacation? Ye wee devil!" Crawford would not succumb to Lanoch's humour.

"Ready your team. We go ashore at the next fishing village. We must be prepared for anything." Lanoch brushed his hands and returned to the other captains. Eva, Spike and George questioned him relentlessly, but they were left unsatisfied.

"Look, if I had ta guess, I'd say it's a snatch n' grab. I doubt we'll find Oswald hidin' in a fishin' barrel," said Lanoch. Spike protested. They were not at war with Sundrithia, yet the Skuas had maintained raids along its coastline, ever since they had sunk Kabil's docked armada. These raids, like their attack on Thindraka, had cost many lives, and soured the Skuas' reputation.

"You wanna have another pop at Merithia instead? Be my guest," said Eva.

"I'll have a pop at you, how's about that?" Lanoch joked, before rallying his companions.

Strange fishing vessels appeared in the distance. Lateen[33] sails soared above the beautiful boats, which swirled into elegant bows. Exotic birds swooped from their spiralled masts in search of fish. A warped jetty snaked towards a village - an isolated paradise - known as Qol. The smell of food filled the air, making their stomachs gurgle. Peculiar trees and fauna had sprouted from the dark sands: sharp reeds and pointed leaves tussled with the breeze.

The jetty was not fit for a galleon, so the Skuas would have to take their skimmers inland. The unit became astounded when Crawford and Grenyard boarded Rias's ship.

---

[33] Triangular sails.

"That spells trouble," Ness grumbled, as she belted herself into a seat beside the bow's gun emplacement. Rob copied her at the stern of HMS Sabre.

"Saddle up," Spike ordered through the cockpit.

Todd squinted as the skimmers were lowered onto the ramps. The cadets would observe their mission from the gunnel. The Skuas pulled their bandanas up, their revolvers clapped as they accepted bullets, sharpened knives became burrowed in holsters and boots. Then, they were cast into the ocean, like wasps leaving the hive. Cannons covered their approach, in an unnecessary show of brute force, by firing warning shots at the surrounding landscape. Sabre Squadron watched as families hurried for the safety of their homes, except for a lone fisherman, who bravely awaited them on the jetty. The cannons fell silent, as Spike pulled up to the construction with Rias in pursuit. The other squadrons would have to wade ashore.

The Sundrithian was unarmed. A sky-blue turban covered his head and a long, fading beard revealed his wisdom. His white robe fluttered in the heat. The Skuas felt cooked beneath their leather coats, black trousers, and waist jackets, yet Spike hurried to greet the man, with one hand on her revolver.

"I know what you seek," he declared. "You'll find no glory here. And no trouble." Spike was shocked and relieved that he could speak Arcayan.

"Go. Return to your home!"

"This is my home. Where else would I go?" the wise fisherman asked.

His face was shrewd and crinkled. Piercings lined his nostrils and ears. She could only imagine what sights his jade eyes had seen.

"You stand before the night devils. They *will* hurt you," Spike warned. She gestured towards Rias's ship, which had docked behind HMS Sabre. Grenyard and Rias stepped onto the jetty. A mob of black coats stormed the dock, as an army of Skuas strode ashore.

"You will bow before me," Grenyard demanded. His tongue squirmed behind his crooked teeth. A fly landed on his eyepatch and sought the smell of rot. Spike dodged aside, as Rias surged past and forced the fisherman to his knees. "You'll tell me how many warriors you have positioned here!" said Grenyard. The man's courage crumbled before his unholy aurora.

He gasped, "How can the sea produce such evil... You have no soul."

He could sense an unnatural darkness in Grenyard, who looked the fisherman in his eyes and said, "I represent unnamed realms. Horrors that can only be witnessed." For a second, the fisherman thought Grenyard would remove his eye patch. His scarred eye was a chilling glimpse of what he had been shown: a realm beyond anyone's understanding. But the peasant did not deserve such an insight. "Captain Rias, make an example of this cretin!"

The fisherman noticed Rias's arctic eyes and said, "You bear the mark of the Veleth-" Rias slit the man's throat and pushed him aside with the sole of his boot. Spike looked away in disgust. Grieved, and stricken with guilt, Ness hid inside the cockpit. It pained her to see Jared's people suffer. Then, Grenyard commanded Crawford to unleash his sailors.

"All squadrons! Clear the village! Bring all captives to the beach for questioning!" Shadows stormed houses, before returning to the beach with prisoners. Men, women, and children were dragged from their homes kicking and screaming. Panic bled from streets and snickets, as Spike led her team down an alleyway lined with baskets, stalls, tanning racks, wind chimes, fine rugs, and toys.

"Watch the roofs!" Spike shouted, as their revolvers scanned potential threats. The alley remained still, except for their boots in the dust. Captain Archer sought shelter and forced a door. The Sabres rushed inside, where a family begged for mercy.

"What the hell is this?" Ness protested. "Oswald isn't here!" Rob reluctantly proceeded into the depths of the abode.

Many Sundrithian dwellings were candle lit, plastered in clay, and built underground where the air was cool. Thatched rugs covered a swept floor, beside hampers, cushions, and figurines. "They're scared!" Ness objected. Two young girls cowered in their mother's embrace. An old woman trembled violently in the corner. Colourful robes failed to sheath them from danger. Ness approached the mother and tried to reassure her. She mumbled a few words in Sundrithian that Jared had taught her, until Rob reappeared with a teenage boy.

Weaving black hair grazed his sloping shoulders. A white thawb[34] covered his body. His face was yet to produce stubble, but the teenager was tall and slender. A candle flickered in his green eyes.

"Ness, tell them they can stay here if the boy comes with us. Tell them we don't mean any harm; that we'll return her son safely," Spike commanded.

"Like the guy on the jetty?" said Ness. She could only utter a few words to ease their suffering and her own despair. Jared was dead and now his stories - his memories - were being trampled.

"We can't return empty handed," Rob said regretfully.

"This is bullshit!" said Ness.

The Skuas left with the teenager in their custody. Ness asked the boy for his name. He was scared but awestruck by her emerald eyes, bloodred hair, alien attire, and Sundrithian tongue.

"Uzair," he replied. His voice had broken, and he was not much younger than Robert. "Please, don't harm my village," he begged.

"Stay back, stay quiet." Ness held his hand and caressed it with her thumb, as a Sundrithian man was booted from his

---

[34] A long sleeved, ankle-length robe.

home. Knees grazed; the father tried to stand, but he was kicked to the ground by one of Rias's men.

"Hey!" Rob shouted, but it was Spike who confronted the unruly Skua by shoving his chest.

The masked thug regained himself before asking, "You wanna join these scum in the dirt?"

"Try it," Spike replied, whilst gripping her hilt. The thug backed away, but he would report her to Rias. The Skuas continued their mission. Sabre Squadron appeared on the beach, where forty people had been rounded up. Grenyard cast his evil eye across a crowd encircled by Skuas.

Then he asked, "Does anyone here know the whereabouts of Vice Admiral Oswald Leonard?" He jabbed the jetty with his cane and raised a small portrait to the crowd. Crabs darted beneath the sands. The villagers wished they could do the same, as they tried to decipher Grenyard's language, but they did not understand his poisoned tongue. After a few seconds, Grenyard turned to his lieutenant, and gave the signal. Crawford hesitated, before authorising the greatest evil.

"Sailors... escort these captives aboard the mothership. Take them to the cells!" The lieutenant had spent endless nights wrestling with his conscious, but he could not defy the chain of command. Shocked Skuas questioned each other, causing the people to stir. Uzair looked to Ness for protection, as Lanoch stepped forth in outrage.

"You've got to be jokin'! These people don't know where Oswald is. They cannae even pronounce his name!"

"That's an order, captain," Crawford said against his will.

"How're we supposed to feed these people!? They're women and children for God's sake!" Their infighting had created a distraction.

"Uzair run!" Ness insisted. But another man had decided to bolt. Rias raised his pistol and shot the runner dead, so Ness grabbed Uzair's hand, to stop him from following her perilous advice. Suddenly, Rias switched targets and fired a bullet at Lanoch's feet! The two warriors exchanged a glare; when

Eva, incandescent with rage, aimed her weapon at Rias. Civilians ducked and quaked before them. Crawford watched in astonishment; irresolute. Rias maintained his stare. He lowered his gun. Then, he marched at Eva. Her finger remained on the trigger, as he approached with haste. But she lacked the courage to shoot. Rias pistol whipped her face, releasing a loud crack. Spike watched in agony as Eva spiralled to the floor; nose bust; teeth fractured. Then, she noticed George, staring off into space. The man was a remnant of his former self. He could not forgive himself for Carla's death, and he could not comprehend their actions in Qol, so he remained still. Their brief mutiny had been crushed. Routed, Lanoch claimed Eva and carried her back to her ship. The villagers were herded onto the skimmers, leaving an entire community destroyed. Ness protested Spike's involvement, despite her own participation.

"What do you expect me to do?" Spike shouted. "Shoot Rias, Crawford, Grenyard?" Rob remained devastated, whilst keeping an eye on their prisoners, including Uzair. Their hands clutched sentimental accessories. Colourful robes brushed their sandals. Knitted turbans, of radiant colours, protected their heads from the sun.

"There are many women and children, sir," said Crawford, as they clambered onto Rias's boat, HMS Claymore.

"As long as they can wield a pickaxe, Lord Whitmore will take them," said Grenyard.

Sartorius and Whitmore had agreed to sneak slaves into Terra province. Coin would wash the hands of corrupt guards and too few cared for damned souls committed to Dead Man's Chasm. All that mattered was increased shipments of hycinthium-lapis, following the failed resettlement programme.

Todd, Abbey, and Gregory watched from the mothership, whilst basking in the sun. Todd had never experienced tropical weather before, so he risked burning his freckled skin. He panicked when Gregory said his nose was peeling. The boy asked if it would stay that way forever.

"You've done it now. It'll drop off eventually," Gregory laughed. Abbey assured Todd that his nose was fine. Suddenly, two gunshots bellowed from the shoreline - Rias had opened fire. The cadets watched in confusion, as their captains turned on each other, and the villagers were loaded onto the boats.

"He's a true captain. Look how the others quiver before him," said Neal, who had appeared uninvited to admire his leader. A breeze surfed his quiff and rustled his trench coat. The others tried to ignore him.

"What do you think they're doing?" Abbey asked, as the skimmers glided towards them through sparkling waves.

"Maybe they're recruiting more sailors, to replace our losses," Todd suggested.

"The last thing this unit needs is more impure blood. We only just got rid of one worthless Sundrithian." Neal was referring to Jared's death. The cadets scowled at him, and Todd thought about his Merithian descent.

"Take that back, Fin," he demanded.

"Make me," said Neal, who loomed over the boy. Abbey ushered Todd away, knowing they had already sworn revenge.

They detected intense fear, as the Sundrithians were escorted aboard. They were huddled together and led into the bowels of the ship, where forty prisoners were packed into three cells. Ness stormed past with tears in her eyes, so Todd asked Rob what was happening. The large sailor looked mortified. Then, Lanoch hurried past with Eva in his arms.

"Go mop the top deck... both of you," Rob demanded. Todd complained, so Rob raised his voice. "NOW!" Startled, the two cadets retreated to find a bucket.

***

A red-rock lamp revealed a creaking passage. Rusted bars and timid hands appeared on the left, where a dozen eyes glinted in the light. Ness called Uzair's name. The teenager wrestled his way to the front of his cell. She handed him some blankets and ships biscuits[35], which he gifted to his elders. The youth was apprehensive and full of questions. He asked why they had been taken, so Ness replied using broken Sundrithian.

"Our leader is missing. His name is Oswald Leonard. Do you know where he is?"

"We know nothing of the man you speak of," said Uzair. His elders murmured and shook their heads. Ness's faint hopes had been dashed. Uzair requested to know where they were heading. The mothership had set sail north, but their destination was unknown. Finally, the boy asked if they would be ok.

"I will see you return home," Ness promised, but the elders expressed mistrust, and she did not believe her own words, yet she was determined to protect the teenager. He reminded her of Jared, as if he were a piece of his memory. Troubled, she headed up top. Spike, Lanoch, Robert and Eva had gathered at the bow. They were stood amidst the black of night.

"Put that light out!" Lanoch whispered. Night hid the awful extent of Eva's bruising. The officers were inspecting the gun decks with Smudge, so the Skuas began their council. Masts groaned above them, as they glided through the abyss, and an unholy choir resonated in the wind.

"Let's face it, we just initiated a bastard slave trade," said Rob.

"We don't know that for sure," Spike argued. She was in denial, so Rob tried to cleanse her delusion.

"Come on. These people don't know a thing about Leonard. Grenyard knows that. It was all a ploy."

---

[35] A biscuit consisting of flour and water.

"We're sailing north as fast as the winds will take us. Anyone would think we've got Tsar Alva of Artrik on board. Aye, this is the work of evil men," Lanoch confirmed.

"What does Oborus want with slaves?" Spike asked.

"Red rock, you know that," said Robert. "It's driven the kingdom into madness."

"There's no guarantee Oborus has decreed this… this could be the council's bidding, or the work of certain lords," Eva suggested. She clutched her jaw and gulped rum. "Either way, Sartorius has sold our souls to the devil. And a devil has command of the mothership."

"We've a decision to make," said Lanoch. An uncomfortable silence consumed them, as a chill ran down Ness's spine. Eva questioned their options. She would be blacklisted for raising her weapon at Rias.

"Cadbey needs the Skuas. The *realm* needs the Skuas, aye. But I'll not serve the malevolent beasts that have hijacked this unit," Lanoch admitted.

"We must find Oswald. He'd put a stop to this, to Grenyard. The unit would return to his command. He's destined to be the king's left hand," said Rob.

"Screw Oswald. He's long gone; the sorry bastard's dead for all we know; probably by Grenyard's hand," Lanoch spat. Eva shushed him quiet, as the gale wrapped itself around them. Oswald had not been seen since their raid on Thindraka. He had disappeared from his cabin without a trace. Pained, Ness suggested they could abscond once ashore. They could track the slaves and set them free before they reached their destination. But they would become fugitives: hunted by a monstrous government or Rias and his men. Spike decided they needed more time. The Sabres felt sick to their stomachs, as they departed a fruitless summit…

Todd kicked a mop bucket across the officers' quarters. Abbey laughed at the prospect of it spilling, so Todd kicked it again. Inevitably, a puddle splashed across the chequered floor, so Abbey gasped mischievously, before flicking Todd with her mop. Grime slicked and dampened the boy's shirt. He gave chase, chucking filth across the passage. Before they knew it, they were stood in front of the great cabin – Grenyard's chamber - where their giggling ceased. Abbey's breathing became staggered, and her eyes became wide.

"Come on, Todd. Let's go to the barracks," she suggested. They remembered the smell of molten flesh and the extent of Grenyard's evil. But Todd wanted to understand the monster. Determined, he pushed the black door wide open, so they could stare inside. Abbey aired her terror.

"If anyone asks, we'll tell them we're mopping," said Todd. He took a deep breath, before stepping inside Grenyard's layer.

A rustic desk, cast from dark oak, stood upon a fine red rug. The rug's triangular pattern was hypnotic and erratic. A grand chair loomed over the desk and a collection of leather-bound books, contorted candles, and ink wells. Curtains half concealed a backdrop of windows, which revealed an empty universe. A red-rock chandelier glimmered. Its light flickered off an elegant drinking globe to the left. A secluded bed could be seen on the right-hand side, but it lacked any sign of comfort. 'Does our commander not sleep?' Todd thought, which made him shudder. Abbey remained in the doorway, to avoid creaking floorboards, and a haunting draft. Todd reached Grenyard's desk. A crude contraption made of sticks lay on the table. It was a bird trap, tied with human hair, but Todd did not recognise it. Other relics could be found: an obsidian tooth, locks of fur, and a twisted jade skull. His tiny fingers hovered, but he did not touch the mysterious items. Instead, he turned to the pile of books. One of the covers looked ancient. Its blemished surface harnessed a strange symbol: the letter A, but its lines continued at the apex to support a red circle, as if it were a stick figure reaching upwards. Todd could not understand the primordial marks scribbled on its pages. Then, he spotted a letter written in Arcayan.

'Commander Blezard,

Your part in Skarsgard's demise resulted in a fitting conclusion, but I trust your raid on Alazi will prove more bountiful and will mirror our recent accomplishment in the port village of Qol. As we return to Arcaya, I must draw your attention to a different matter. Oswald has-'

Abbey yelped as a large figure stomped towards them. Frightened, Todd clutched his mop and pretended to clean.

"What in the blazes are ya doin' in 'ere!" Rob asked, as he appeared in the doorway. Abbey gawped up at him like a cornered animal, so the sailor turned his attention to Todd. "Out of here, now!"

"But, sir," Todd pleaded. "This letter mentions the man you've been looking for." Rob marched over and attempted to snatch his mop, so Todd ran around Grenyard's desk.

"We can do this the easy way or the hard way!" said Rob. He stopped to admit, "Curses, I sound like my father." The boy reached across the table and snatched the letter, before encouraging Rob to read it.

"It mentions Oswald!" Dubious, Rob leant across, took the document, and peered at its text.

'Oswald has defected to Merithia. I prefer the rumour that he died by my hand. However, my eyes[36] have spotted the scum arranging safe passage from Krith[37] to Keldor[38] and onto Varlden Halsstad. I'm awaiting further word, but I have

---

[36] Grenyard's eyes are Skua agents or mercenaries operating inland for the R.B.S.

[37] Krith is a small island republic located in the southern archipelagos of Sundrith. This trade hub attracts drifters, merchants, and forces from all over Arcaya, Scavana, Sundrith and beyond.

[38] Keldor is a protectorate of Merithia, an ancient gateway to Sundrith and Scavana, but the Skuas have ensured it is a burden to protect.

dispatched mercenaries to return his head, and ensure that the traitor poses no threat to our supremacy. Word cannot reach shore of what the cretin has done. Ensure this letter burns.

Supreme Commander Grenyard.'

Silence engulfed the great cabin. Todd asked what the letter meant. Rob was overcome by a mixture of concern, hope, and resolve. He insisted it was nothing, before frantically replacing the items.

"So, you're not mad?" Todd asked, still clutching his mop like a weapon.

"No, now let's get out of here whilst we have the chance!" They bustled outside and closed the door behind them. Crawford was stood in the passage! Rob, Todd, and Abbey gasped in unison. The obnoxious lieutenant asked them what they were doing.

"Apologies, lieutenant. I caught these nippers mopping the great cabin. When I said, 'clean the whole place head to toe,' I didn't mean Grenyard's quarters!" Rob took the opportunity to clip their ears, causing them to whine. Fortunately, Crawford's sympathy for Abbey prevented him from commenting any further. After an awkward pause, Rob escorted the cadets away. The lieutenant made his way inside the great cabin. He skirted its perimeter, before approaching the desk, where he also read Grenyard's letter.

Chapter 13
The Hand that
Holds the Sickle

Don prayed that the black bear would not reappear, as he carried Niamh through the snow. She kindly assured him that leopards or wolves were more likely to eat them. Her hands gripped his cape, so Don could focus on his footing. Poles anchored him, and his snowshoes provided poise, whilst his visor deflected the chilling breeze. After a painstaking hike, they reached Scathed Sickle Pass, and the scene of a bloodbath. Niamh insisted that Don put her down so he could search for Laith. He investigated black glaciers, the carcase of a big cat, and the frozen husks of dead men.

"He's not here," Don confirmed. "And neither's Rorik." He peered over the ridge, where he glimpsed a manmade avalanche, below the mist. Fearing the worst, they made their way into the pass. They discovered a carriage: obliterated by boulders. Niamh despaired at the sight of mangled horses, so Don set her down once more. Shivering, he continued his exploration. But he was not the first to inspect the disaster. The footprints of a lone wanderer had been preserved, and a soldier had been dragged from the wreckage. He wondered what words the crystalized corpse had uttered before achieving death. Had it confirmed Alan's survival? Had it seen Laith rise? Regardless, they were nowhere to be seen. Blood led away from the crash. And a satchel containing medical equipment had been cut from a steed. Bandages remained strewn across the floor and further prints lured

Don's eyes down the Scathed Sickle Pass, where something glinted in the snow. He hurried forth and discovered his Skua dagger, which Laith had borrowed.

"Laith came through here alright!" he told Niamh. "It doesn't look as if he was followed. And the rest of the convoy made it through." They hoped Rorik had slithered into the mountains; never to be seen again.

Don had barely slept; but he proceeded with Niamh on his back, haunted by the thought of Rorik, until the gorge was behind them. A crisp valley lay ahead. Its winding track was barely visible. Timeless mountains loomed either side, whilst observing their struggle. Niamh talked, so she could ignore her burns.

"You're wasted as a sailor. You should've been a pack horse." Don was too exhausted to reply, but he appreciated her humour. Petrified coppices could be seen on the slopes. Fieldstone walls and shrines of Allód began to appear. Suddenly, Don fell to his knees, so Niamh rolled into a white cushion. Panting, he scooped the snow into his canteen. Then, his quaking hands removed a parcel of meat from his jacket, which he shared with her.

"This valley is dead," said Don. He struggled to chew his meal. He had prayed in vain for a carriage to appear that would take them to safety, warmth, and a soft bed.

"Ye of little faith," said Niamh. "Reckon they've got a bed for the night?" A smoke trail had risen above the trees. Don sighed in hope and pessimism. Arca's farmers were isolated, suspicious folk. They worked hard to appease the rebels, as well as King Oborus. They were not to be trusted. Niamh could hear his cogs turning.

"We don't have a-"

"Choice, I know," said Don.

"You're the daft bastard who brought me along," Niamh chattered.

Don told her, "Shut up and eat your meat." Then he hoisted her onto his back. They trudged across a field of deceased crops and buried dreams.

Lopsided walls and contorted beams supported a thatched roof. The grim dwelling boasted a porch, but winter had rendered it useless. Eyes observed their approach through broken shutters. Logs lay out front, beside a frozen trough. Don placed Niamh down, before turning towards the cabin. A draugr had appeared in the doorway, brandishing a sickle.

The man's cut, shaven head resembled a skull. His brown clothes were tattered. A torn scarf failed to warm his neck. And a filthy cloak wrapped his fragile frame.

"Ebony knights?" the man asked, after observing Don's helmet and visor. Don refused to answer, so the man blurted, "Do you have food?" Don nodded cautiously. An odd silence followed. Then, a shadow whispered something in the man's ear. "Then come in," said the farmer in a hoarse voice. "We'll see to your needs." The skeleton stepped aside to reveal a frost-bitten passage. Don hesitated, before carrying Niamh inside.

The atmosphere changed, as a mother and child greeted them. The boy was wrapped in a sheepskin blanket. Ribbons of golden hair surrounded his face. His mother wore a patched dress and a similar cover. A solemn expression ruled her face, yet she had tied a scarlet band around her frayed hair. She led them through a carpenter's kitchen, where rustic furniture covered a slabbed floor. Candles tried to dispel the gloom. A smouldering hearth, packed with pans, yearned for attention. A bed awaited them in the back room. Its walls had been insulated with horsehair, but a breeze seeped through the gaps. Don feared a lice infestation. Still, he thanked the frightened family, before tending to Niamh.

"I know how to change a dressing. Get acquainted with our hosts. Ask them if they've seen Laith, and then we'll get some rest." She looked ghostly. Tails of hair escaped her hood.

Wheezing, Don entered the living area and removed his helmet.

"Is she well?" the farmer asked.

"She's fine," said Don. "She just needs rest." He was reluctant to reveal the extent of her wounds.

"In that case, what supplies might ye be carrying?" Don sighed, unfastened his satchels, and dropped them on the table. He revealed food parcels taken from the Abalone Guerrillas. The mother covered her mouth and wept.

"Have it," said Don in pity and tiredness. He knew they could hunt game on the road.

"No time to cry woman. Let's get a stew on the go and show our guests we're humble folk," said the farmer. Don asked where he could sleep, so the man pointed him to the same back room.

"There're spare blankets under the bed. No funny business. This is a blessed house." Don laughed at the prospect.

Then he asked, "A Sundrithian passed through here. Have you seen him?" The family became quiet. Then, the man shook his head. Don was unconvinced. Still, he showed his gratitude by bidding them goodnight, and hauled himself back into his timber chamber. Niamh was already asleep. He sighed in relief, whilst admiring her peaceful look.

"It's the floor for me then," Don muttered. He would have to sleep on the ground, like a dog wrapped in plaids, but it trumped sleeping in a cave surrounded by murderers.

***

A prod woke Alan from his slumber. He coughed and looked at the guards.

"End of the road, Mr Witherow," said Drew.

"Aye, let me get me things together," Alan said with a smirk. A shallow beard had formed beyond his moustache. His hair remained slicked back, but it would not hold for long.

"It's been a pleasure," Drew admitted.

Their carriage climbed towards the capital of Arca province. Arced turrets rolled across its white walls, where cannons glistened in their crenels[39]. Metallic domes, doors, chimneys, and statues represented all the wealth in Arcaya, by giving the citadel a golden aroura. Birds sprang from garlands and balconies, where the wealthy could enjoy sundown. Plumes rose from a ticking display of new inventions, powered by the wonders of hycinthium-lapis. The city's tram system no longer relied on struggling horses. Instead, electric charges enabled carriages to glide as if they were alive. Oborus desired a replica system in Cadbey, but its streets were too crowded. Drones were barely feasible. Still, he was reluctant to resettle citizens in Arca, despite pressure from the lords to increase the production of hycinthium-lapis.

Alan found himself inside another cell; banished from the world. A bucket was his only company. It remained beside a stone bed. 'At least this cell has a window,' he thought, but it was beyond his reach, and allowed winter to drift between the bars. Rage burned in his veins. His family name had been destroyed, the Skuas remained tainted, his only son was in peril, and there was nothing he could do.

Alan lost hope and track of time. Then, keys signalled the arrival of a visitor. 'Arthur!' he thought. He gripped the bars of his cell. To his disappointment, Lord Whitmore appeared.

The smell of stale smoke and whisky followed his waddle. The pig coughed to clear his gullet, which Alan found offensive. Goldleaf decorated his vest jacket, which was bursting at the seams. A velvet suit expressed his wealth. Bracelets contained the finest gems his men had scraped from the planet, and his fingers brandished golden rings. A monocle magnified his eye, which looked Alan up and down.

"The great Alan Witherow, in chains, I never thought I'd see the day," Whitmore laughed. His cheeks joggled as he

---

[39] An indentation in the battlements of a fort or castle.

spoke. "Look at your pyjamas. Look how silly you look." The man hacked to clear his neck of excited phlegm.

"Have you simply come ta gloat?" Alan growled.

"No, no. I've come to offer you my condolences, as one minister to another. Except, you're not a minister are you… and you never were," said Whitmore. Alan had been a guest, or a voice of reason, at the king's table. The lord came closer, so he could reveal his secrets. "You're a remnant Alan, of a bygone era. The kingdom is going nowhere, a bit like you. The monarchy has got us locked in a prehistoric cage, and it cannot continue. Johnathan Ackerley is presumed dead. This has only increased support for a worker's republic, and an end to Oborus, including his personal guard the Skuas, who are most likely responsible for his death," Whitmore explained.

"I sort reform, hence why I'm 'ere," Alan stated. "I've always praised the council. I simply want the Skuas ta be what they once were. Honourable protectors, not night devils. Sartorius has gone senile, and evil men sit under his wing."

"Then join us," Whitmore demanded. "I'm offering you a choice. You're the admiral our nation needs." Alan's indecision caused him to pace, but he knew where his loyalties lay.

"I will not go against my oath, my king, or my unit. Besides, you don't represent the people. All you care about is the riches in these hills, at any cost," Alan answered. Whitmore had been exposed. The king was unwilling to resettle civilians in Arca, the church was influencing its followers to stay in Cadbey, and Whitmore was struggling to maximise his profits by obtaining hycinthium-lapis. But a republic, in the form of an oligarchy, would give him ultimate power.

"Then you'll be serving our new central committee from the mines of Terra province. The state is grateful, Alan." The lord began his departure. "I wield the worker's sickle. We will end Oborus, and we will end this perpetual war with the Kingdom of Merithia. The Skuas will be tried for their crimes… I'm sure Todd's life will go a long way towards trade negotiations." Alan waited until Whitmore had left, before slamming the bars of his cell. In a moment of despair, he prayed once more for his only son, and that help was on the way.

***

"They're burning, they're burning!" Niamh shouted. Fretting, Don staggered to his feet. He pivoted to see Niamh: panting, sweating and confused. She had awoken from another night terror. Fortunately, morning had broken. Don assured her that it was just a dream. But a sickness was rising within her. He quit their room in search of food. The farmer's wife greeted him from her seat at the table. A nervous silence followed, so Don apologised for any distress Niamh may have caused. The haggard woman forgave him by offering a bowl of wheat pottage.

"I can't," said Don against his will.

"Aye, we don't have much. A meal before noon is a privilege I rightly pray for, every night. But you are our guest, which is all the more reason why you must eat." She pushed the bowl towards him, as if it were cursed. Don gave in to his hunger. His hands dwarfed the carpenter's cutlery.

"Thank you," said the gentle giant. "May I ask your name?"

"You can call me Elgar. My husband is William, and our boy is Aaron. It was his thirteenth birthday two moons ago, not that we could treat the boy. It has been an unforgiving year and God knows winter has just begun," the woman explained. Elgar's tongue was animated, but her body seemed bound. She remained perched upon a crooked stool, where she refrained from making eye contact.

"I hate to be rude-"

"You mustn't go," she interrupted. "Not until our boy has returned." Don became confused.

"I was going to let my companion eat. And ask if you have an outhouse?" A beetle scurried across the table, which the woman splattered with her hand.

"We've had problems with the outhouse," the woman said fiercely. She removed a handkerchief and wiped her palm. "But my husband has dug a new stench pit at the bottom of the field. You can do your business there." Don swallowed his disgust, before revisiting Niamh. She swiped the bowl from his hand and began slurping.

"I'm gonna look around. I won't be long."

"Trouble?" she asked.

"Just wait here," Don requested.

"Are you takin' the piss?" Niamh replied, eyeing her leg. The adventurer headed through the kitchen and stopped at the front door, where a frame of light beckoned him.

"Where's Aaron…Your boy?" Don asked. Elgar had not moved, as if she were shackled.

"He's a good lad. Aye, he's a good boy. He's gone to fetch herbs from the woodland to heal your lady's wounds. As part of our gratitude. So, hurry back now, don't dally." Her words were believable, but Don was unconvinced. Something was amiss. He exited into a white dimension. A low sun caused the snow to glare, as Don made his way around the cottage. Chickens could be heard clucking, one longhorn cow stood in a barn built for greater numbers, and a dapple-grey horse had been tied to a post, beside a waterlogged forge. The farm was failing, but it was yet to see its final days. Crows ignored Don, whilst foraging for seed. He followed the treeline, and footprints, until he reached a hellish ditch. The gaping cesspit challenged his senses; but he persevered by turning, dropping his trousers, and pulling his cape from danger.

"Don't mind me my good sir," William yelled, as he appeared with firewood. Shocked, Don yanked his trousers up.

"You could have looked the other way!" Don shouted. Cold fingers struggled with his belt.

"It would be rude for a man not to greet his guest on such a fine morning as this!" William seemed agitated, and unaffected by winter's chill, which had paralysed the woodland behind him. "I insist you come with me at once, and I shall prepare a fire, and breakfast!" He scratched his head to eliminate lice. Don declared he had already eaten, but the frail man persisted.

So, Don asked, "Where's your boy?" Surely, he had not been left in the woods, where wolves prowled and bears foraged.

"Mucking out the stables," William answered.

"And what about the herbs?" The farmer turned with a look of worry and confusion on his face.

"We must go back, immediately. We must go now." He grabbed the sailor. Bewildered, Don knocked the firewood from under his arm. William stumbled and glanced across the field. People were approaching the farm. A line of wolf pelts and axes signalled Rorik's arrival. Three menacing huskies led the way. Aaron was sat atop a horse beside them.

"BASTARD!" Don spat. He grabbed the farmer by his neck and lifted him into the air. William squirmed in his cloak.

"A man has to feed his family!" he pleaded through rotten teeth. Furious, Don choke-slammed him into the cesspool. Then, he sprinted towards the farm like a bull. The guerrillas recognised his immense stature. Bullets caused the snow to spit around him. Don screamed Niamh's name, as he burst into the house. Elgar resembled a statue. Her eyes remained fixed on an empty table, so the veteran ignored her.

"We've been sold out!" said Don. He swooped Niamh onto his shoulder. Then he hurried back outside and found the dapple-grey horse. The guerrillas were less than a hundred meters away, so Rorik released his hounds! Axes reflected the sun towards their prey. Wild eyes homed in on the restrained mount. The imperilled horse panicked, but Don and Niamh were able to climb aboard. Then it reared, as a hatchet pierced the barn beside them. Niamh revealed her revolver and fired.

Their attacker crashed into the frost, as a husky hurdled a fence. Sweating, Niamh shot the beast, before it could clamp the ankles of their steed. They took off. Rorik's charge had ended in vain, but his dogs pursued them into the forest. Niamh tried to reload, as thunderous hooves caused her bullets to spill! A ravaging husky increased its speed. Its teeth snapped at their horse's tail; the beast could taste victory, until a bottle shattered its nose. A whine signalled surrender, and the veterans disappeared into the distance.

"That was the last of the good stuff," said Niamh. "Do you think Laith passed through there?" she asked, as they continued weaving between the trees.

"There was no sign of him," Don replied. "I bet the farmers let him slip through their fingers before Rorik could reach them. We were supposed to be a consolation prize."

As their horse stormed north, they doubted they had seen the last of Rorik. They hoped Red Rock Citadel would provide all their desires: a warm bed, a hearty meal, and Laith, if he had survived the tundra. Until then, tarnished knight of the realm, Sir Alan Witherow would remain in chains, and the kingdom would edge closer towards peril...

***

A cloaked figure made its way around the back of The Earl's Corner Club. Clinking chains and bracelets suggested it was an apparition. Then, its cane thudded a cellar door, which opened suddenly.

"Lord Whitmore, we were beginning to think you weren't coming," said the gate keeper.

"Nonsense, get out of my way," the lord demanded. He descended from the cold and made his way into a smoke-filled chamber. A group of surreptitious characters cheered his entrance from a plethora of barrels, crates, and stools, where lamps shimmered in the damp stones of an arched basement. Lord Ross removed his hood and greeted his fellow peer.

Professor Langley also showed his respect, but his anxiousness kept him seated. Satisfied, the lords requested silence. Their periwigs and monocles set them apart from the mob.

"Your respect is greatly appreciated, and it is reciprocated," said Whitmore, as he gathered a speech. "Workers built this kingdom. Workers conquered Arcaya. *Workers* have died protecting it. Not the Skuas, who stole their greatness. Not the night devils, who've spent decades bloodying the seas at our expense! Not the monarchy, which has bathed in glory, whilst its people struggle in the dirt." Whitmore's audience jeered as he jabbed his jewel encrusted cane. Smoking pipes glowed in the gloom like fireflies. "You, the backbone of this land, are the future. A future without archaic laws and perpetual war; a future that offers better rights and security for all!" An anarchist stepped forth from a band of Ebony Knights. His name was Oscar Aggus, and he had come on behalf of his father, Peter Aggus who was leading their warriors in battle.

The rebel removed his cowl to reveal a wide jaw, wiry sideburns, and a wild fringe. His unbreakable stare had been carved from a block of stone. Unfamiliar allies struggled to see past his youth. But his shrewd eyes demanded respect from anyone who crossed him.

"And what of our security? Will we finally be left alone to live as we please? As promised when you first met with my father?" Oscar quizzed. An axe handle protruded from his grey cloak.

"Have you not done as we've asked?" Whitmore asked rhetorically.

"We lost many knights battering Fort Dry Cote, but it's drawn soldiers away from the capital," Oscar declared. "My father has travelled north to retrieve men and speak with the Abalone Guerrillas, as requested… They will join our cause." The young knight was mistaken. His father, Peter Aggus was dead, and Rorik's Abalone Guerrillas were chasing Alan.

"Then you shall be rewarded. For our time has come. We've been blamed for the drone bombings that struck Cadbey. The late, Johnathan Ackerley was taken from us, and he will not be the last, unless we strike now! The king believes we're a threat. Let's prove him right!" Langley passed him plans coined from his brilliant mind.

"Three weeks from today, our compatriot knights from Ebonshire will assault the house of Ernest Bestla. They will capture the right hand of the king, and they will force him to sign over the command of all land forces to Major Ricktor Lucon." Whitmore stared at a cloaked man, in a dark corner of the basement.

Lucon was short, clean shaven and unsettling. He removed a smoking pipe from his crooked mouth. The psychopath had been promoted for his cruelty on the battlefield, and he bore the scars of his insanity. Burnt skin, formed from specks of shrapnel, covered his face. Further scratches dashed his buzzcut. Sharp, green eyes exposed his madness. His blue tunic was scuffed and dotted in unkempt medals. White trousers fed into his tattered boots, and a black cloak hung around him. Lucon was Artayan. He despised himself for surviving the battle of Porth Trefilian, but Lucon despised Bestla more, for forcing his bloodlust on his own people. Traumatized, he had come to detest the Oborian empire, the Kingdom of Cape Cadbey, and its ruthlessness towards any whisper of independence.

"Every party member will be expected to rise. Flood the streets with chaos! Let Oborus shiver under the sickle!" Whitmore's army pledged their allegiance with further cheers. "Bestla's forces will be stretched thin. He'll be wanting reinforcements. However, Lucon will take his men and enter the palace, under a guise to protect the king. But the king will be forced to abdicate, and a reformed council will take charge. And that ladies and gentlemen is how you achieve a coup."

"And what if Bestla doesn't sign over command," Oscar jabbed. He doubted Bestla would succumb to a rebel from Ebonshire.

"Get creative. He'll have his family with him," said Whitmore.

"I want Bestla. Me and Oscar will swap," Lucon suggested. Baffled, Whitmore looked to his peers for support.

Langley explained in an elegant manner, "Lucon, we need your men inside the city walls. If you attack Bestla's residence, his guard will immediately suspect a coup and lock the city. Whereas Oscar's assault will simply look like a stab at revenge. If anything, it will pull further soldiers from the capital. Plus, no one will suspect your troops when they enter the palace. We can keep the death toll to a minimum."

Lucon scoffed, "What kind of an uprising would that be?"

"A civilized one," Langley murmured.

"And what of Sartorius?" Lucon asked. "The king has two hands!"

"I have a friend who would like to deal with the admiral, and replace him," Whitmore replied. "Drink now to the coming of the new dawn!"

Once more, Whitmore became an apparition. He quit The Earl's Corner Club and boarded his horse drawn carriage. It carried him through a dense fog, away from Cadbey, towards a forgotten harbour, where he would meet the admiral's replacement.

Chapter 14
Shattered Oaths

Lanoch could hear footsteps. He scrambled for his knife, causing his hammock to spasm. Large hands grabbed his jacket and shook him!

"Oswald's alive, the bastard's alive!" Rob whispered.

"For God's sake, Simmo ye wee prick! I could eh stabbed ye, ye stupid bastard, get off me!" Lanoch batted his hands away. Rob eagerly repeated himself. "Aye, sure, a part of him lives on in all our hearts," Lanoch replied. Rob checked their surroundings, before describing the letter Todd had found.

"Merithia…. So, he's abandoned us… for the reaches of Scavana?" Lanoch muttered. Rob had acknowledged the fact Oswald was alive. But Lanoch was more focused on his shocking betrayal.

"We must find him. Oswald will put a stop to all of this!" said Rob.

"Have ye lost your mind? If what ye say is true then Oswald has joined the enemy, and broken his oath," said Lanoch.

"I don't believe, for one second, that Oswald would defect. There must be another reason for his departure. Something to do with Grenyard I would bet! And there's no guarantee he's reached Scavana if that's where he's heading. The letter mentioned Krith and Keldor-"

"Simmo, my dear boy," Lanoch patronised. "Say we make it ta Krith or Keldor in one piece, and the vice admiral isn't there… what then?" Both knew they could never return if they deserted. There would be no turning back.

"Then we continue…," said Rob.

"And sail into the lion's den?"

"If that's what it takes," Rob murmured.

Lanoch sneered and said, "I wish I was still young and foolish. Get some rest." Defeated, Rob disappeared into the creaking darkness. He found his bedsit: a mattress beside the root of a mast. But he would struggle to sleep. The ship groaned and cannons rustled beneath their chains. Rob asked himself what his father would do. He wished he could seek Don's advice from an armchair beside their fireplace. An image of his father reading, and sipping port beneath candlelight, brought him comfort. Don would often read to him whilst he was ashore. Little did he know, his father was amongst the Abalone Mountains, battling frost and fatigue. The same tenacity still burned in his veins.

Lanoch huffed as boots approached once more.

"I thought I said get some rest," he said. He opened one eye, as the ridge of a blade lifted his beard, and grazed his neck. Arctic eyes glinted at him through the blackness.

"I marked the girl, but I did not mark you," said Rias in his harrowing voice. "Time and again you test my patience… No more."

"Slit my throat and I'll cut your balls!" Rias looked down to see a knife pressed against his crotch. Before he could react, a revolver smacked the back of his skull. Rias collapsed to the floor in a heap!

"Hurts doesn't it," Eva spat in revenge. She had eyed Rias from her bedsit, and she knew evil was at play. Distressed, Lanoch quit his hammock and hurried his first love away.

"We're leaving, now! Once Rias wakes, we're dead meat," he stated. They reached Rob's mattress. The teenager hoped Lanoch had changed his mind about Oswald, but his blood ran cold when he learned what had happened.

"Look, ye can stay. It's me n' Eva who Rias has got it in for. But there's no tellin' where any of this al stop. So, d'ye still wanna jump ship or not?" Lanoch asked. They had not decided their course, or whether they would search for Oswald, but time had betrayed them. Its hands were ticking, and they were nearing Arcaya's shores.

"I'm not leaving without Todd," said Rob.

"Aye, or wee Abbey. We'll grab Spike n' Ness. You get the nippers!"

Rob cast his blanket aside and rose to his feet, before asking, "Do you think Spike will join us? Will she lead us out of this?" Spike was a Skua by choice. She embodied the unit, and she had doubted the establishment of a slave trade. Yet, above all else, she was loyal to the Sabres. Thomas Witherow was the only captain she had ever admired. He would not have stood for Grenyard nor Rias's ways.

Lanoch added, "Aye, Spike hates Rias more than any of us. They're like bulls in a cage... She'll do what's right." Eva nodded in agreement, believing Spike would follow what remained of her fractured heart. Rob nodded, subconsciously pinched himself for doubting her, and left the gun deck. Lanoch grasped Eva's shoulder. He thanked her ardently.

"I'd let you thank me properly if my face wasn't so bust up. For old times' sake," Eva smiled.

"Aye, there's no kissin' that lump better, but hold that thought," Lanoch joked. They shared a firm embrace, before disappearing through the shadows.

Rob prayed that Rias was still comatose. The demon could be hunting him amongst the impenetrable blackness. Afraid, he swept past sleeping souls and deep shadows, downstairs and through jagged hollows. Finally, Rob reached the barracks. He yanked a curtain aside and nudged Todd and Abbey awake. They questioned what was happening, which triggered Neal to stir.

"Grab your things, quickly!" Rob ordered. The cadets wriggled in their hammocks and slipped into their clothes, but they were taking too long. The giant placed Todd and Abbey under his arms.

"What are you doing!?" Neal asked before they could leave.

"Training," said Rob, but Neal could tell he was lying. The audacious teenager gripped his poncho.

"Liar, what's going on? Where's Captain Rias and the others?" Rob demanded he 'let go' and 'return to sleep' but Neal persisted. "What's going on, Simpson? You're not much older than me, or wiser, I demand an explanation!" Rob thought twice, before nutting the boy unconscious! Neal thudded the floor, which caused all the curtains to open. The cadets arose like imps in the night, so the giant fled with Todd and Abbey under his arms.

Spike and Eva had already reached HMS Sabre, but Ness had taken a detour. Lanoch called her name without raising his voice.

"For Pete's sake, Nessie, we have ta go!" She would not leave without seeing Uzair one last time. Panting, she grasped the bars and summoned him. The teenager pushed to the front.

"Uzair, we're leaving... Lanoch, get the keys!" she ordered.

"What!? I don't have the keys - Ness, this is madness, we cannae take them. If ya save one ya have ta save them all!" Ness demanded to know where the keys were, but Lanoch was right. "Ness, we have ta go!" he pleaded by gripping her shoulders. Heartbroken, she returned to Uzair.

"I'm sorry. For all of this. We're abandoning the night devils for what they've become... for what they've done. I promise we'll put a stop to this... We'll see each other again." But her words felt empty.

"Please, don't go," Uzair pleaded, so Lanoch pulled her away. They met Rob, Todd, and Abbey on deck, before striding towards Spike and Eva. The full moon had escaped the clouds, and all was bathed in a silver glow. Smudge approached them with a suspicious look. Eva did her best to gain his assistance, but fear bested the wary sailor.

"I won't stop you. But I cannot assist you," said Smudge. "May the waves carry you." The sailor faded away.

"Bastard," Eva grunted, but his calmness had been observed by the other Skuas on deck, so they would not interfere. He had bought them valuable time. Fretting, Rob passed the children to Lanoch, who placed them aboard Spike's vessel.

"We're low on supplies, captain," said Ness. Spike's skimmer rocked indiscreetly, as they hurried back and forth. She was too preoccupied to recognise her new given rank.

"We don't have time. We'll have to make do," she said.

"STOP THOSE TRAITORS!" Rias bellowed from the quarter deck. Their stomachs turned, as a hundred gargoyles became animated. The monster marched towards them with death in his moon lit eyes. Skuas dropped from nets and masts to prevent their escape. Smudge was forced to abscond.

"GO!" Eva screamed. She leapt at a winch and released its lever. Chains clinked and her comrades staggered, as HMS Sabre began to lower. Lanoch demanded she jump aboard, but their boat was not descending quickly enough. Desperate, Eva booted the winch! Three kicks broke the contraption, before one of Rias's men could tackle her to the ground! Lanoch yelled Eva's name, as their boat fell and smashed the waters below, forcing them to their knees. He clambered to his feet and began scaling the chain like a beast!

"EVA!" he roared. He could not abandon his first love, but Spike grabbed his legs against her will.

"Away! I can save her," Lanoch yelled. Their struggle sent them hurtling to the ground. Rob grabbed the wheel and started the engine, as Ness detached the hooks from their ship. They knew Eva was lost. Spike and Lanoch looked up in despair. Rias had forced Eva to her knees before a full moon, and a row of hostile silhouettes. Frayed bicorn hats and torn coats bent in the wind.

"THIS IS WHAT WE DO TO TREACHEROUS FILTH!" Rias thundered. They watched in horror, as he yanked Eva's head back, and slit her neck, before throwing her overboard. A cry forced its way out of Lanoch's throat, as Eva's body struck the waves.

"I could have saved her!" he screamed. Spike tried to restrain him, but he escaped her grapple, lunged at the nearest Gatling-gun, and fired into the abyss. Rage flickered in his eyes, as the mothership became a monolith in the distance. Finally, the turret clicked dry of bullets, the barrel stopped spinning, and Lanoch stopped screaming.

Spike returned to her feet and shouted, "Are you finished!?" An awful silence followed a waste of ammunition. Spike's heart had also been ripped apart. She wiped her bloodied lip, which had been caught in the tussle. Shattered, Lanoch stepped away, and threw himself down on a seat.

"I'll kill that bastard, if it's the last thing I ever do," Lanoch growled.

Spike had to take charge. She ordered Robert to kill the engine, so they could listen for the sound of skimmers. Peaceful waves rustled beneath their ship. The wind wheezed as it tried to avoid them. They were not being tailed…

"Are you ok?" Ness asked Todd and Abbey. Unsure, they nodded and shivered. They were growing used to Death and its constant presence.

"Are you?" Todd asked Ness. She fought her tears, smiled politely, and squeezed his shoulder. They could not be allowed to drift. And their emotions could not be allowed to take control.

"We must head south," Rob insisted.

"Oswald isn't in Krith," Lanoch spat.

"Oswald?" Spike questioned. Ness raised her head in hope. Resolute, Robert described the letter Todd had found. The boy confirmed it was true, before battling his thoughts.

"If I hadn't found the letter, Eva would still be alive," he blurted. "We wouldn't be banished!"

"Nay, Rias was already comin' for us, lad. You've done no wrong," Lanoch assured him. Abbey held Todd, as Lanoch removed a canteen of whisky from his coat and began drinking. Torn, Spike took a moment to consider their options.

"We must head south!" Rob shouted once more.

"Shut up!" Spike ordered.

Returning north would be suicide. They would be portrayed as deserters throughout Arcaya – traitors who had shattered their oaths. And they could not head west. Word of their crimes in Qol would spread throughout Sundrithia. Even if they could survive the deserts, Sundrith offered no solace. Above all else, she feared for the lives of Todd and Abbey. Maybe they should have left them behind. Afterall, they had already failed to protect them from the horrors of war. She also feared for the wellbeing of her mates. Thomas, Jared, Carla, and Eva had already fallen. But sailors need a purpose.

"We head south," she decided. Lanoch scoffed at their madness.

"What about the slaves. What about Uzair?" Ness asked.

"There's nothing we can do. But we may be able to save the next village. We find the vice admiral, we regain our honour, and we put a stop to all of this." Spike restarted the engine, so Rob took his seat at the stern.

"Regain our honour, by seeking a deserter?" said Lanoch.

"Grenyard and Rias are behind this. Oswald will have the answers," said Rob.

Ness wrapped the cadets in blankets, before resting with them beside the cabin.

"Well, it's not like we've anythin' ta lose," said Lanoch. He mourned Eva's death and took another gulp of whisky.

"Spoken like a true Sabre," Ness muttered, as Lanoch was no longer the captain of Rapier Squadron. He cast his eyes to the countless stars above them.

Todd asked, "Does this mean we're pirates now?"

"Aye, we may as well be," said Lanoch.

"No," said Spike. "We still have a code. And a mission."

"Don't worry, Todd," said Abbey. "As long as we stick together, we'll be ok. We'll find Oswald." Todd nodded in agreement, before staring up at Zora's star.

"You two try and get some sleep," Rob insisted, so Ness placed her arm around Todd and Abbey, to help them settle.

The Sabres set off across the Aeternum Ocean to find Sir Oswald Leonard, the truth, and a way to stop Grenyard; oblivious to Alan's imprisonment, their parents' endeavours, and the fall that awaited their kingdom…

***

The sun fell from a blistered sky. Finally, it disappeared beneath the horizon. Blackened waves lapped the lonesome wharf, where silhouettes watched the sea. Whitmore had waited almost a week. His patience was waning when suddenly, the mothership appeared in his telescope.

"It's about damn time!" He could not bear to spend another night in Seddon, a failed port town. But he became anxious, as the galleon drew near. Its mutilated faces resembled a ghost ship. Spectres lingered behind torn sails and distorted timber. Then, Grenyard appeared on deck with Rias by his side. They observed Whitmore, as a bridge was lowered. A stream of slaves and skuas followed its course. The lord was not impressed.

"Most of these are women and children, commander!" he shouted. Famished souls were ushered past him. Uzair was one of them. His white thawb had been ruined, and he squinted as the light hurt his eyes.

"Then let the sea take them," Grenyard suggested. Typically, Whitmore looked to one of his personal guards for support. The guard's eyes begged for mercy, so Whitmore conceded. Crawford watched in shame from afar, as their cargo was delivered. Guilt and fear plagued his mind. He had read Grenyard's letter, confirming Oswald was alive; he had seen Rias kill Eva, the night Sabre Squadron had fled; and now he watched as Grenyard conspired with Whitmore and his crimson guard[40].

"I have a proposition," Whitmore shouted.

"Then I suggest you board my ship," said Grenyard. Whitmore stared up at the haunted vessel. Then he observed his delivery. The wharf gave way to a stretch of ruins, where his slaves were hustled into a line of armoured carriages. Satisfied, the lord swallowed his fear and staggered up the bridge. Rias's eyes were cold, unnatural, and fierce. His tampered top hat and satanic scar also made Whitmore feel uneasy. And Grenyard did not seem of this world. A black heart beat beneath his chest.

Whitmore repeated himself. "I have a propo-"

"To bargain with the devil, is to sell one's soul," Rias muttered. Whitmore fell quiet, as the wind tugged at their clothes.

"This man has no soul," said Grenyard, who stared through the foul lord.

"I have... a proposition... a revolution is unfolding, gentlemen. In a few days, the king will be forced to abstain, Bestla's Oborian Guard will be no more, and a new workforce will begin flooding the state with red rock." Grenyard and Rias remained silent. "I know you were denied the position of vice admiral. Which is why I want you to *have* the seas; to continue our operation. Everyone knows Sartorius has lost his mind, and he cannot remain as the king's left hand." Grenyard was impressed by Whitmore's knowledge and nerve. The republicans had spies everywhere.

"That and he won't betray the king," said Grenyard. He considered slaying Whitmore where he stood, in line with his oath. But Grenyard nor Rias would be rewarded by the current

---

[40] Like the Oborian Guard, the Russam Guard have sworn allegiance to the king. However, they were formed and are funded by Lord Whitmore. They have been dubbed the Crimson Guard due to the colour of their uniforms.

regime and their sights were set on power. "How do I know you won't betray me?" Grenyard took one step forward, so Whitmore could smell his putrid breath. The lord carefully collected his words. His new order would not survive without the R.B.S; to protect its shores from Merithia, and to provide its mines with slaves.

"Because the Skuas *are* Arcaya..."

TO BE CONTINUED IN

SABRE ©

PART II

THE RISE OF THE NIGHT DEVIL

ACKNOWLEDGEMENTS

If you enjoyed this book, I would be greatful if you could publish a review on Amazon or Goodreads, etc. Every review makes a huge difference. Thank you.

SABRE PART I is dedicated to my Nana, Jill Wendy Wood, who would let me use her computer to write my stories after school. She is always in our hearts.

I have taken much inspiration from my Grandad, Robert Geoffry Atkinson, who served in WWII in Europe and India. He spent his later years up and down the motorway in his lorry, making deliveries. May he rest in peace after a long, adventurous life.

I would like to mention my friends at the Green Room in Altrincham, with special thanks to Rob Hull for his support. Everyone's creativity and energy has driven me.

To my wife, Jennifer Wood. Thank you for your love, and for enabling me to explore my passions and express my creativity.

I would like to thank my parents, Stephen and Sally Wood for their continued support and encouragement. And my sister, Laura for all the treasured childhood memories, which have inspired my writing. Finally, I would like to thank further friends and family for your kindness, support and feedback. You know who you are, and those who read the draft trilogy: Uncles Richard and Michael Atkinson, Poon Simpson, Matthew Owen, Freya Barnett, Alan Wood and Kieran Boland.